"I didn't mean to offend."

"No?" Rhea questioned. "Maybe you didn't, Stephen, but you didn't stop to think about your actions. Your sort never does."

His gray eyes dilated dangerously and he drew himself up stiffly. "And what do you mean by that remark?"

Rhea's cheeks grew hot. She'd gone too far and she knew it. "Nothing, I...I..."

He grabbed her elbow and she froze.

"Tell me what you mean by my 'sort'?" he demanded harshly.

She stared down at his fingers gripping her flesh, and added "violent" to his long list of faults. Wrenching her arm away, she lifted flashing eyes.

"The sort," she burst out, "who wants all the pleasures of the bedroom and none of the responsibilities!"

MIRANDA LEE was born and brought up in New South Wales, Australia. She had a brief career as cellist in an orchestra, and then another as a computer programmer. A move to the country after marriage and the birth of the first of three daughters limited her career opportunities to being a full-time wife and mother. Encouraged by her family, she began writing in 1982. She favors a well-paced what-happens-next kind of story, but says what matters most "is that my books please and entertain my readers, leaving them feeling good and optimistic about love and marriage in our present topsy-turvy world."

Books by Miranda Lee

Don't miss any of our special offers. Write to us at the following address for information on our newest releases.

Harlequin Reader Service
P.O. Box 1397, Buffalo, NY 14240
Canadian address: P.O. Box 603,
Fort Erie, Ont. L2A 5X3

MIRANDA LEE

an obsessive desire

Harlequin Books

TORONTO • NEW YORK • LONDON
AMSTERDAM • PARIS • SYDNEY • HAMBURG
STOCKHOLM • ATHENS • TOKYO • MILAN

Harlequin Presents first edition December 1991
ISBN 0-373-11419-2

Original hardcover edition published in 1990
by Mills & Boon Limited

AN OBSESSIVE DESIRE

CHAPTER ONE

RHEA was late. She raced into the back of the church and opened the lid of the upright organ. Thank the Lord the bride was late as well! With a ragged sigh of relief she sat down and concentrated on sorting out the sheets of music she would need.

'Excuse me . . .'

Rhea controlled the surge of impatience at being interrupted and glanced up, only to have the blood drain from her face.

'I'm sorry to bother you,' the man standing on the other side of the organ said, 'but I have a message from the bride's mother.'

Rhea could not believe her eyes. It couldn't possibly be! Not the *same* man. Not *here*, at a small wedding on the outer fringes of Sydney, in an old, almost dilapidated church. This was the last place on earth such an individual would be!

But it *was* him! There was no doubt in her mind.

'. . . Miss . . .?'

He was puzzled, no doubt, by her open-mouthed surprise.

Surprise? That was a ridiculous word to use to describe her feelings, Rhea conceded. *Shock* better explained the sensations which even now threatened to embarrass her with devastating force. Her stomach was in instant knots. Her heart was pounding madly. And a mortifying heat was beginning to claim her normally cool cheeks.

His puzzlement became concern. 'Are you all right?' came the kind enquiry.

Rhea's mouth snapped shut. She struggled for composure and appeared to win. 'Sorry,' she apologised, though curtly, 'for a moment I thought you were someone else. But I was mistaken.'

A smile lit up his thoughtful face, lifting his straight black brows and transforming the cool grey eyes into warm wells of charm. It rocked Rhea considerably, but this time she didn't show it.

'I'm glad,' he returned. 'I wouldn't have wanted to be the man you thought I was. You looked positively terrified for a moment there!'

Terrified . . .

Yes, he was right—he did terrify her.

But *why*?

'Mrs Gabroni wanted to know,' he went on smoothly, 'if you could play Gounod's 'Ave Maria' while the couple are in the sacristy signing the register. It's a favourite of hers. Do you know it?'

Rhea's affirmative was made through dry lips.

'She also asked me to give you this envelope. It contains the agreed payment for today.'

He placed it on top of the organ, a flash of diamond and gold sparkling from one of his fingers. Rhea found her gaze travelling from his carefully manicured fingertips across the crisp white cuff of his shirt, then up the arm of the superbly cut black jacket.

No rented suit, that, she decided shakily. It had been made specially to fit his superb body so that not a crease formed around the strong neck and wide shoulders. And the material was a silk blend, of that she was certain. A rich man's dinner suit.

But then she had known he was well off, and successful, this man who terrified her.

'Thank you,' she managed with eyes already dropping. To gaze into that face again was out of the question. She had made enough of a fool of herself already.

But when he kept standing there, not moving away, obviously still staring down at her, she was forced to look up. 'Yes?' she asked, swallowing.

His eyes flicked assessingly over her, making her stomach muscles tighten again. Rhea knew what he was seeing, knew she was an attractive woman with her big blue eyes, shapely figure and dainty oval face. Her hair too was a drawcard, for it was long and thick and dark, given to fluffing out on to her shoulders before falling halfway down her back in a wild mass of loose curls. She usually tied it back some way, but she'd been running late, and had decided to leave it.

An unfortunate decision, she groaned silently, for the man standing before her was gazing at her abundant tresses with speculation in his eye. Was he wondering what it would look like spread out on his pillow?

Rhea was shocked by her train of thought, and the fantasy-like mental image she was having of herself in his bed. It rattled her, almost as much as the man himself. And yet he wasn't the first man to come on to her in the six years she had been widowed. Not by a long shot.

Till recently she had worked as a cashier in the local supermarket—the only job she could get as an untrained ex-housewife—where she had endured countless propositions from the sales representatives who called. At first she had been upset by their blatant attempts at familiarity, but she soon learnt to fend off their passes with skill and tact.

She knew, however, that the disturbing stranger smiling down at her at this very moment was not the sort of man to be fended off easily.

'I was admiring your hair,' he said quite openly. 'Don't ever get it cut.'

Such a personal comment instinctively made her bristle. 'Really? I was thinking of doing just that, in fact,' she lied.

'Don't,' he reproached. 'To do so would be a crime.'

Another smile accompanied his words, once again sending her pulse-rate into an agitated syncopation.

She glanced around in nervous defence, searching for an escape from the distress he was causing. Her veins seemed charged with electric currents, the nerve-endings along her arm prickling her skin into goose-bumps. 'I'm sorry, but the bride will be arriving shortly,' she excused herself hastily. 'I must get ready to play.'

'Of course,' came the silken reply. 'And I must find a seat.'

He flashed her a parting smile, undaunted, it seemed, by her apparent lack of response. Would he come back to try again after the ceremony?

The thought unnerved Rhea considerably, and it was with apprehension that she watched the tall, elegant figure wander down the aisle. When he stopped and slid into an empty row on the right she held her breath in anticipation of his glancing back at her, but he didn't.

Instead he settled himself comfortably in the corner, sitting half side on, one arm curved lazily over the back of the ancient pew, his long fingers tapping idly on the wood.

Her eyes were compulsively drawn to the unforgettable lines of his profile, so distinctive with its strong, almost sharp nose, its squared jawline and prominent chin. As she studied him his chin tilted up slightly so that the glossy black waves lapped over the startlingly white collar. He looked incredibly handsome and totally self-possessed.

Not so herself. Rhea was a jumble of nerves. A mess!

The intensity of her agitation now brought frustration and anger—but more at herself than at the man. Why should this particular male make her feel like this? So churned up, so upset . . . Why?

It wasn't as though he meant anything to her. He was a stranger, for heaven's sake. Oh, yes, she had seen him before. *Twice*! Which she supposed was astonishing in itself. But he hadn't seen *her* on those occasions, let alone spoken to her. She didn't know his name. She didn't know where he worked or where he lived. She really didn't know anything about him, except what she'd been able to deduce. That he was successful in whatever he did for a living—and with women.

Of course the status quo had changed now. He *had* seen her this third time, and he *had* spoken to her. In fact, he had shown quite clearly that he found her attractive. Nevertheless, why let that unnerve her so? Wasn't she used to deflecting that type of male interest?

Rhea forced herself to keep looking at him, his face, his hands, his body, his mouth . . . forced herself to finally face the feelings that even now were welling up inside her again, feelings which she could no longer pretend she didn't recognise, despite their newness.

It's because I want him too, came the slow admission. And it took her breath away.

Yes, that was it, she confessed to herself, slowly, dazedly, hardly daring to face this incredible truth. His name, his position, his background, didn't seem to matter. She just wanted him.

She shuddered, her eyes falling to the keyboard. She was appalled by her desires. Appalled! She had never wanted a man like that before. Never. Ever!

And the unfamiliar feelings terrified the life out of her.

'Mum!'

Rhea blinked. She heard Emily's voice dimly, but her mind was still in turmoil.

'Mum, the bride's waiting for you to start,' Emily whispered urgently.

Rhea finally registered her attention on her daughter's worried frown, pulling herself together sufficiently to flash her a reassuring smile. Yet her fingers felt wooden as they plopped on to the keyboard, amazing their owner by finding the right notes out of sheer habit.

The whole congregation rose for the bridal chorus, watching the bride's entrance with rapt attention. Rhea neither saw nor heard a thing for the entire time it took to complete the piece, staring blinding down at the keys till her fingers finally came to a halt.

She lifted nerveless hands and sagged into the stool before slanting an anxious glance over at Emily, afraid her daughter might have noticed her odd behaviour. But no, Emily's gaze was fixed in childlike wonder on the ceremony.

Rhea closed her eyes, hoping perhaps to wash her mind clear of any more disturbing thoughts. But it was the worst thing she could have done, for it catapulted her memory right back to the very day . . . the very moment . . . when she had first set eyes on the man.

It had been nearly six months previously—a cool windy day in August. Rhea had travelled by train into Sydney to keep an appointment at an exclusive boutique in the Centrepoint shopping complex. Her objective had been to sell some of her original handmade garments, lovingly crafted from the mohair she spun and dyed herself, a hobby which she hoped to turn into a steady source of income. Being a widow with a mortgage and a ten-year-old daughter to support was a constant battle of balancing the budget.

She had come out of the boutique on cloud nine. She had sold everything and had a contract for more! The job behind the check-out counter was already a bad memory. Of course, she would continue playing the organ at weekend weddings, for that would provide extra savings for Emily's future education.

Pleased and excited, Rhea had decided to treat herself to a cup of coffee and a sandwich at one of the exclusive coffee lounges high up in the Tower. And it had been while she sat there sipping her *cappuccino* that she had first seen the man.

He had been a couple of tables away. With a woman—a lovely young woman with soft brown eyes and stylishly cut short blonde hair. But of course it had been *he* who had first drawn her eyes, with his striking colouring and sheer male beauty. The rich black hair and deeply tanned complexion seemed spotlighted by the paleness of his light grey business suit and crisp white shirt. He was the most elegantly groomed man Rhea had ever seen—not to mention the handsomest.

She had stared and stared and stared, so much so that at one point she had had to look down quickly when he had glanced her way.

There had been no mistaking the intimacy between the couple. The smiles, the low laughter, the touches, all bespoke a relationship beyond mere friendship. And of course there had been the present he had given her —a bracelet, or a watch. Rhea could not quite see which. The girl had thrown her arms around her lover's neck and kissed him. Rhea had finally got up and left, almost running away from the most peculiarly distressing feelings that had invaded her while watching them.

The second time she had seen him had been less than two months later, in early October. Her mother and stepfather had been going on a package tour of New Zealand with some other members of their bowling club, and, since Rhea hadn't been back home to Kiama to visit for quite a while, she had offered to drive in to Mascot airport and see them off.

The plane was slightly delayed and during the unfortunate wait conversation soon dried up, as it did whenever Rhea and Bill were forced to endure each other's company for longer than a few minutes.

Their relationship had always been strained, Bill having married her mother when Rhea was at the vulnerable age of twelve, and only a year after her father had been killed in an industrial accident. Rhea had been shocked by the way her mother seemed to like Bill's physical attentions. They were always touching and kissing, embarrassing her so much so that she had kept to her room most of the time.

She had struggled through years of resentment and the feeling that she had become the outsider in her own home. It was one of the reasons she had fought so hard to maintain a secure and loving home life for her daughter after Milan's death, with as few changes as possible. She had vowed never to bring a stranger into her home by marrying again; she didn't want Emily ever to feel as she had done.

So Rhea had been glancing around the busy airport terminal in agitated silence when her eyes landed on the very same man she had seen in the coffee lounge.

He had been coming out of the VIP lounge, looking executive-suave in a navy pin-striped suit, one arm wrapped possessively around the waist of a statuesque blonde. Not the same one he'd been with before, Rhea had noted with surprise, then cynicism. So, she'd thought, he was one of those . . .

This woman had been older, around thirty, with startlingly made-up eyes in a vibrant face, a sexy mouth and a spectacular figure. He had seemed to be reassuring her about something, holding her close, talking softly in one ear.

Rhea had stiffened as she watched the man lift a hand to gently touch his companion's cheek. And when his mouth had bent to the woman's in a long, lingering kiss, she had spun away, feeling both embarrassment and a sharp stab of distress. She had determinedly not looked back, surprising her stepfather with a sudden spurt of animated conversation. Of course, when she had finally glanced over her shoulder the man and woman had disappeared.

At the time, Rhea had not recognised the emotion that had twisted inside herself. But now, as her eyes opened to scrutinise the man in the pew once more, she realised what it was she had felt. She had been jealous! She—Rhea—had wanted to be the woman in his arms, having him touch *her* cheek, kiss *her* mouth . . .

Suddenly he looked back over his shoulder towards the back of the church, and penetrating grey eyes clashed with wide blue ones. Rhea blinked, knowing she should tear her gaze away, fearing what he was already seeing in her expression. But she could not. Instead, she kept looking at him, and when he smiled at her the temptation to smile back invitingly was almost overpowering.

She stopped herself just in time, dropping her eyes to stare fixedly down at her hands in her lap, several seconds passing before she realised that her hands were shaking, literally shaking.

Oh, God . . . What on earth was happening to her?

Yet being appalled at herself did seem rather silly, Rhea decided with a flash of frank reality. So she was attracted to the man—wildly attracted. Was that so wrong, so bad? She was twenty-nine, for pity's sake. And six years a widow!

She knew full well what other widows in her position would do. They certainly wouldn't be having any qualms. They would lift their faces, smile, and give the man the message, pronto!

But you're not other widows, her conscience inserted fiercely. Not at all. Don't pretend this is just a normal, healthy frustration that you're responding to. My God, woman, be honest! You've never even *liked* sex! So why are you lusting after this man?

'I now pronounce you man and wife.'

Rhea came back to reality with a jolt, fumbling to start up the organ again to play the requested piece. The guests chattered quietly amongst themselves, and as the strains of Gounod's 'Ave Maria' wafted over them, each haunting chord clear and precise, none would have envisaged the fragile state of their player. Once again Rhea found the notes with an automatic skill, her smooth performance belying the fact that her inner composure was totally obliterated.

When the signal came to change the music to 'Here comes the Bride' her heart began pounding along with the beat of the music, but not from gaiety. The thought that at any moment the object of this unexpected and obsessive desire would stop to talk to her again was throwing her completely. Just go away, she willed wildly as she played. Go away!

The happy couple walked past and everyone else began pouring into the aisle behind them. Don't look up, she kept telling herself frantically. Just keep playing. Keep playing. Maybe he'll walk on by.

But out of the corner of her eye she saw a pair of black trouser legs stop beside her, and instantly her entire body moved into a disturbingly breathless state.

Her response bothered her terribly. She didn't *want* to want this man. Not at all. She was happy and content with her life as it was. And while she might be inexperienced—her husband had been her only lover—she was not so naïve as to believe a woman could tangle with the likes of *this* Romeo and get away scot-free.

Rhea dragged in a steadying breath, set her teeth firmly in her jaw, and with dogged determination kept playing. She kept playing till the church had emptied, stopping only because it was both stupid and futile to go on. For he was still there, one elbow leaning against the top of the organ, watching and waiting for her to finish.

'You play quite beautifully,' he remarked as she bent to switch off the electricity. 'Where did you learn?'

She closed the lid and stood up. 'A nun taught me,' she said, giving him the benefit of only the briefest glance before she began shuffling the various sheets of music into a neat pile. Without any encouragement he was sure to depart, she reasoned. Most men did.

'Ah, yes, the good sisters. They always have an ear for music. And talent.'

Rhea's chin snapped round. If there was one thing that really aggravated her it was flattery. Her organ playing was competent, and that was all. If this man thought he could . . .

He smiled at her and any retort died in her throat.

'I . . . I'm not that good,' she murmured.

'Mum, the bride's leaving,' Emily called out from where she was standing in the doorway. 'Aren't you going to come and see?'

It all happened so quickly. The man glanced first at Emily, then down at the third finger of Rhea's left hand. She had never taken off her wedding-ring, the gold band having protected her sometimes from unwanted advances. It had never occurred to her that one day it would protect her from a wanted one.

He glanced back at Emily and his face changed, from an engaging smile to a frown. He made some excuse about having to get home and left before Rhea had a chance to correct his natural assumption that she was a married woman.

Which was just as well, she reasoned a split second later, an ironic grimace twisting her mouth. One miserable smile from him and she'd been about to make a complete fool of herself!

She snatched up the envelope still lying on the organ and stuffed it into her large bag, along with the sheets of music. 'Come on, Emily.' Her tone was brusque. 'We might as well go home too.'

And with a swish of her black pleated skirt she grabbed Emily's elbow and left, totally ignoring the groups of guests lingering in the churchyard. She turned her head neither to left nor right, propelling her daughter over towards her small van.

'Are we in a hurry or something?' Emily asked as they both climbed into the hot, stuffy cabin.

'I have a lot to do before school starts again on Wednesday,' Rhea explained, winding her window down noisily. 'One of these days,' she added irritably, 'I'll be able to afford a car with air-conditioning.'

The engine fired on the third try, then lurched through the churchyard towards the narrow exit. A sleek silver sports car had the same idea at the same time.

Rhea braked, as did the sports car. She knew before she looked directly at the driver who it was. The car fitted the man.

Once their eyes actually met he gestured gallantly for her to go in front of him. But she declined, sending him ahead with an insistent wave. He nodded appreciation and accelerated quickly away, his preoccupied expression showing her that he had already forgotten her. With hands clenched around the steering-wheel Rhea watched till the powerful vehicle disappeared over the crest of the hill.

'Mum? You can go now—he's gone.'

Rhea congratulated herself on the way she proceeded smoothly out of the bumpy driveway. There was not even a hint of the emotional chaos her daughter's words had evoked.

Gone . . .

She would never know his name, never see him again . . .

I should be grateful, she told herself. Relieved. Ecstatic. Out of sight was out of mind, wasn't it?

A rueful smile touched her mouth as she turned the van towards home. What point was there in fooling herself? Rhea knew she would not forget him, or the needs he had evoked in her, in a hurry.

CHAPTER TWO

RHEA swung the van into their driveway, carefully negotiating the planks of wood that served as a bridge across the culvert. The dogs were barking and jumping up and down in their wire run as she came to a halt under the carport attached to her fibro cottage.

'I'll let Bobby and Dolly out,' Emily said eagerly.

'Make sure the chooks are away first,' Rhea warned. Emily hated locking the dogs up, but Rhea knew that it was a case of 'better to be cruel to be kind.' Their two dogs were Australian terriers who just adored chasing little things that moved. And Rhea's biggest and best hen had just hatched a dozen chickens.

Rhea was busily opening the doors and windows in the stuffy house when she was drawn outside by a commotion. Once free, the dogs had raced up the back yard and into the goat paddock and were making a real racket, barking madly and racing in circles round the old shed where Rhea kept the hay and oats.

A snake, came the immediate thought. There'd been one in there last year and Rhea had nearly had a heart attack. Dolly, who was a fearless little creature, had killed it.

'I'll go and see what's bothering them,' she said. 'Emily, you stay inside!' Without thinking of her own safety she picked up a spade and ran.

'Get away from there, Dolly,' she shouted as she scrambled through the strand-wire fence. 'Oh, you crazy fool, get away!'

Bobby, who was by far the bigger dog, but inclined to be timid, clustered around Rhea's feet, almost making her trip over. 'Stop being so brave, Bobby,' she growled, then laughed. 'Oh, good grief! One killer dog and one coward!'

But she loved the dogs dearly. Gran had bought them for Emily a couple of Christmases earlier, and, despite their shortcomings, they were part of the family.

Not only that, Dolly was a good money-spinner, having produced a couple of pure-bred litters to Bobby, and at this very moment was looking pregnant again. Rhea hadn't told Emily, but she intended to use the money from this litter to buy the pony that had been her daughter's dearest wish for some time.

She finally extricated Bobby from her ankles, raised the spade in readiness and crept around the side of the shed. Her heart was thudding madly, for snakes terrified the life out of her.

With her arrival, Dolly had quietened, which didn't exactly help Rhea's nerves. The silence was ominous. She took the final petrified step that brought the inside of the stable into view, surprise making her nearly drop the spade on her foot.

A little girl of maybe seven or eight was sitting on the sack of oats, staring at her and looking even more terrified than Rhea. That she had been crying was obvious.

'For goodness' sake!' exclaimed Rhea, then recovered sufficiently to lean the threatening spade against the side wall. 'What have we here?'

Bobby had joined them now, curiosity getting the better of his fear. When he sniffed the little girl's feet, she drew them up quickly and whimpered.

'It's all right,' Rhea soothed, coming forward to squat down in front of the child. 'They won't bite. They just want to meet you.'

She looked into the tear-stained eyes and saw sheer misery. Her heart turned over. 'What's wrong, sweetie? Can I help? Are you lost?'

Rhea knew all the local children and this little girl was not one of them. Of course, she could have recently moved into the area; there had been a lot of buying and selling since the Government had decided to build the new international airport only a few miles away.

'Do you live near here?' she asked. 'Would you like me to ring your parents?'

Silence. But the child had flinched at the mention of her parents and the tears were rolling again.

Rhea battled to control a growing fury. What sort of people would upset a child this way? And what sort of treatment exactly had she been subjected to?

She did not let the child see her anger. Instead she asked gently, 'How about coming down to the house with me for a cool drink? It's terribly hot in here and you look as if you've walked a long way.'

And that was the understatement of the year! The child's arms and legs were scratched—no doubt from climbing through barbed-wire fences—and her dress was dirty and torn.

Rhea's observant eyes went over the dress again and she frowned. It was an expensive garment, made from fine material with expert craftsmanship—not the clothing of a poor, underprivileged child.

'Coming?' she suggested, and held out her hand.

The child hesitated, then slipped down from the sack, curling grubby fingers into Rhea's slender palm. The trusting gesture squeezed at her heart.

Immediately the two dogs rushed up to the child, jumping up and down on their short sturdy legs, begging for a pat, but the little girl cringed away. Not used to dogs, Rhea thought. Certainly not country born and bred. 'If you give them a pat,' she explained quietly, 'they won't keep on bothering you.'

The little girl did so, tentatively.

'My name's Rhea, by the way,' she told the child as she took the small hand again and began heading back to the house. 'And what should I call you?'

Two big grey eyes blinked up at her. 'Laura. Laura Hatfield.'

'A pretty name for a pretty girl.' And she was too. Like a doll, with delicate features, a porcelain skin and jet-black curls.

Emily was waiting at the back door, looking anxious and puzzled.

'We have a visitor, Emily,' Rhea said. 'Her name's Laura. Laura, this is my daughter Emily.'

'Hello,' Emily tried, but Laura said nothing.

'Come on,' Rhea went on brightly, 'let's go inside and have a Coke.'

Emily beamed. It wasn't often Rhea allowed her to have soft drinks. 'I'll get us some glasses,' she offered eagerly.

Laura drank the Coke, but that was the extent of her co-operation. She sat at the kitchen table, the empty glass in front of her, not saying another word. All the prompting in the world hadn't got any extra information out of her. But at least she'd stopped crying.

Rhea decided to try a different tack. 'Would you like to change your dress, Laura? That one needs a wash, don't you think? Your mother wouldn't be too happy to see such a beautiful dress ruined, would she?'

That did it. Though Laura's reaction was not exactly what Rhea had in mind. The child burst into tears again, this time sobbing her heart out. Appalled that she had upset the little girl, Rhea did her best to comfort her, cuddling her close and stroking the glossy black curls. 'Oh, Laura, Laura my dear, I'm so sorry! Whatever did I say?'

'I haven't got a mother any more,' came the choked reply between sobs. 'She . . . she died last year . . . and . . . and *he's* going to send me to boarding school. My mother said she'd never do that . . . never ever! But *he* doesn't love me . . . He hates me . . . and I hate him too now!'

'There, there, my dear, I'm sure he doesn't hate you, whoever he is. Are we talking about your father?'

'Yes . . . Mr Chase.'

Rhea pulled back and frowned down at Laura's crumpled face. 'Mr Chase? But surely your father's name would be Hatfield?'

'No.' Laura blinked and sniffled. 'He . . . he never married my mother.'

Rhea gritted her teeth. 'Didn't he now?' she said tightly. 'And where does your father live, Laura? Around here somewhere?'

The little girl nodded.

'Do you know the address?'

'Lot four, Mountain View Road. It's a new house,

two-storeyed.'

'That's the place above the old dairy, Mum,' Emily joined in. 'You remember the one. We talked about how quickly it went up.'

Rhea certainly did remember. A rich man's house. A rich man who hadn't bothered to marry his daughter's mother, and who was now packing the unwanted offspring off to boarding school because she might get in the way of his lifestyle.

A storm was brewing inside her. There was nothing that enraged her more than injustice and unfairness and cruelty, particularly to children!

She stood up and strode across the kitchen, snatching up the pencil and notepad she kept near the phone. But before she returned to the table she scooped in a steadying breath. Keep the anger for the father, she told herself. No point in upsetting the child further.

'Could you write your phone number down, Laura?' she asked calmly enough. 'I'll have to ring your father—you must realise that.'

The child's eyes rounded in alarm. Dear God, Rhea fumed inside, she was terrified of the man! 'Don't worry, Laura, I'll smooth everything over and see what can be done about your going to the local school with Emily. Would you like that?'

It was heart-rending to see those grey eyes light up so. 'Could you? I mean . . . Oh, that would be wonderful! I like living out here better than in the city. And I did so hate the thought of leaving Mimi.'

'Mimi?'

'My pony. I only got her last month and I haven't even learnt to ride her yet.'

A pony . . . Something twisted inside Rhea. It annoyed her that this so-called father would probably have bought his daughter a pony without giving it a second thought. Anything to keep the kid busy, she imagined him saying. While her own Emily had wanted a pony for years . . .

'Do you really have a pony?' Emily asked, without a trace of envy in her voice, only interest. 'What colour is it?'

'Sort of grey.'

'Why don't you take Laura to your room, Emily, and have a chat while I ring her father, OK?'

The girls were gone in a flash and, despite her inner anger, Rhea felt nervous. She did so hate personal confrontations, hated the way they left her feeling sick inside. But she felt she had to do something positive for Laura, not just hand her back to this unfeeling man.

She dialled, her fingers trembling slightly. The phone began ringing at the other end. Ringing and ringing and ringing. Five, six, seven, eight times. Answer the damned thing, you . . . you . . . Simon Legree!

'Stephen Chase here.'

A lump filled Rhea's throat now that he actually answered.

'Hello? Is anyone there? Speak up, for God's sake,' the voice snapped, 'or damned well hang up!'

The impatient, harsh tone was exactly what Rhea needed to fortify herself. She coughed and straightened. 'Would I be speaking to Laura's father?'

There was a moment's hesitation before the voice said stiffly, 'You would.'

'Then you might like to know,' she went on archly,

'that at this moment your Laura is here in my home crying her eyes out, utterly distraught and miserable.' Which was only a slight twisting of the truth, she justified to herself.

'Don't be ridiculous, woman! My Laura is upstairs asleep in her room. You must have some other Laura.'

'Oh, really? Are you quite sure about that?'

She heard the sharp intake of breath down the line. 'Hold on . . .' The sound of running upstairs was clear as a bell, as was the sound of his angry return. 'Let me get this clear,' he roared down into her ear. 'Is this some sort of ransom demand? Have you kidnapped my daughter?'

Rhea was floored. And speechless.

'Speak up, woman! Are you or are you not making some sort of criminal demand?'

'Of . . . of course not!' she blurted back.

'Then why have you got her? If you hurt one hair of my daughter's head you'll wish you'd never been born!'

Rhea felt her face burning with indignation and embarrassment. 'Mr Chase! I didn't take your daughter— she ran away and I found her! And if you th——'

'Would you kindly tell me exactly who and where you are?' he cut in harshly.

'I will if you'll let me finish a sentence,' she snapped. 'My name is Rhea Petrovic, *Mrs* Rhea Petrovic, and I repeat, I didn't have anything to do with your daughter's running away from home, but from what I can see you have a very unhappy girl here, Mr Chase, and one whom I'm loath to return to you, in the circumstances!'

She could feel his fury across the air-waves. 'I'll give

you just ten seconds, Mrs Povlovic or whatever your name is, to tell me where you live, or I'll ring the police.'

'Petrovic,' she repeated with a desperate return to calm. She had sudden visions of squad cars descending on the house, an event which would keep the neighbours in gossip for years. 'There's no need to get in a flap, Mr Chase. Your daughter is quite safe with me.'

'I have only your word for that, madam, and, since I don't know you from a bar of soap, I'm hardly mollified!'

Rhea dragged in a deep breath and counted to ten. Mollified, indeed! How pompous could you get? 'Then I suggest you come here and judge for yourself. Go all the way to the bottom of your hill,' she informed him stiffly, 'then turn left. Take the first turning on your right—Creekbed Close. My place is at the far end of the road, number sixteen. The number is plainly painted on the post-box.'

'I'll be there in five minutes,' he rapped out.

'You do that,' she snapped, only to find that the phone was already dead in her hand.

'Of all the . . .' Rhea's hand was shaking as she dropped the receiver back into its cradle. Who did he think he was, accusing her of being a kidnapper? And who did he think he was that his daughter would be kidnapped? Some darned multi-millionaire or something?

She felt a queasy pang in her stomach. She conceded the possibility that Mr Chase might be quite wealthy, but so what? She gave a brave and defiant toss of her head. Did that give him special rights? Did that excuse his high-handed rudeness? No! Definitely not!

She began to pace up and down the kitchen, her mind racing with both apprehension and indignation. She kept reminding herself that she had never been nor ever would be impressed by the very wealthy of this world. They seemed to believe that they could step outside the rules of society and get away scot-free. This man had fathered a child without marrying the mother, and now expected some boarding school to do the parenting for him. What kind of man was that?

Her lips curled up in contempt as she pictured the type. Ruthless and egotistical, self-centred and arrogant, a man who gave no quarter and took what he wanted, a man who demanded and expected to be obeyed, a man who was undoubtedly used to people grovelling at his feet, saying 'Yes, sir, no, sir, three bags full, sir.'

Rhea's nicely shaped mouth set into a stubborn expression as she ground to a halt. He needn't think he could push her around. She had learnt to stand up for herself since being widowed, something that continually surprised people who had known her as Milan's quiet, slightly nervy wife. Not that she had been frightened of Milan, Rhea reassured herself. Though now that she thought about it, he had sometimes displayed a quality of suppressed violence about him.

She recalled one night early on in their marriage. They had gone to a local function where she had had a couple of glasses of punch. The hidden alcohol in it had made her more outgoing and vivacious than was her usual way, and several men had paid quite a bit of attention to her. Milan had been furious with her when they'd got home, accusing her of making a spectacle of herself. He had reduced her to fearful tears, then taken her with uncharacteristic roughness. In the morning he had apologised but the incident had lingered in her mind, and she had been so very careful after that when in company not to do or say anything that would provoke his jealousy.

'Was my father at home?' a tiny voice asked.

Rhea whirled round to see Laura and Emily standing in the far doorway. Laura was clutching Emily's Cabbage Patch doll.

'Yes, sweetie, he was.'

'Oh . . .' she frowned '. . . it doesn't matter, then. I meant to tell you he might still be out. Mrs King was minding me till he got home. I was supposed to go with him this afternoon, to the wedding, but I got sick at the last minute . . . I mean, I *said* I was . . .'

All the breath had been punched out of Rhea's body. 'Wedding?' she repeated weakly. 'Did you say wedding?'

'Yes, the man who does our garden was getting married today. It was at the old church down the road. I guess my father didn't go on to the reception. I guess he came home to check on me . . .'

'It was probably the wedding you played at, Mum,' Emily said quite naturally. 'Laura's father must have been one of the guests. Fancy that!'

No . . . Rhea clenched her fists for control. No, it wasn't possible . . . It couldn't be . . .

With an awful feeling of fate closing in, she stared into Laura's eyes. They were the same shape, the same grey. Then her scrutiny shifted to Laura's hair. It had the same blue-black luminescence, the same thick texture.

A shiver raced up and down Rhea's spine. Oh, hell!

'When's he coming?' Emily asked ingenuously.

Rhea found her voice with difficulty. 'Soon . . .' She gulped. 'Very soon.'

CHAPTER THREE

RHEA tried not to think of what lay ahead. 'Girls, I think it would be best if I went outside and spoke to Laura's father alone. You can watch TV, OK?'

Laura was only too pleased not to have to face her father and Emily seemed delighted to have company. They raced off together, leaving Rhea standing nervously alone in the kitchen.

She smoothed the pleats of her black skirt down with clammy palms, checked all the buttons on the plain white blouse, then was attempting to pat her hair into some sort of order when she heard the low rumble of a car coming down the road. Coming fast.

Her stomach turned over. She knew, no matter what the odds, that Laura's father was the same disturbing man. There was a weird sense of inevitability about the situation. Nothing she could say or do would change it. And nothing she could say or do would change how he made her feel. She would have to deal with him—and herself—as best she could.

She moved through the side door just as the silver car swerved from the road into her driveway. It careered across the culvert, missing her post-box by mere millimetres, clouds of dust billowing out behind as the wide wheels ground to a halt in the dirt.

The two dogs went hysterical, sensing the threatening nature of this arrival. Bobby put on his fiercest façade, actually baring his teeth.

Rhea tried to resurrect her earlier indignant anger,

thinking that would be her most effective weapon, but she went numb when she saw the now familiar figure climbing out from behind the wheel. He was still dressed in that immaculate dinner suit. *All* of him was immaculate, from the crisp bow-tie right down to the shiny black shoes.

It struck Rhea forcibly as she watched him stride boldly towards her that if she had to be victim to an uncontrollable, unreasoning passion she could not have picked a more dangerous subject to long for. Here was a man who had women coming out of his ears! Rhea doubted that the young lady in the coffee lounge was old enough to have been Laura's mother. And as for the blonde at the airport? Somehow she couldn't see such a vibrant-looking individual as having been the mother of someone as shy as Laura.

No . . . This Mr Chase was undeniably a man who loved variety. Not for him a settled, committed relationship. If he ever sensed that there was a pretty little widow down the road yearning for him, he would gobble her up and spit her out for breakfast.

Yet he was looking anything but a devil-may-care womaniser as he drew near. His expression was grim and formidable, and an increasingly nervous Rhea realised that this confrontation wasn't going to be easy.

He totally ignored the barking dogs at his heels, so much so that they eventually fell by the wayside, probably as stunned as she was every time she set eyes on the man. A host of feelings warred inside her, not the least an alarming loss of confidence.

But at least she was not letting it show. She stood straight and tall, arms folded, chin up, eyes steady.

He drew to within an arm's length of her, his frown giving way to an astonished recognition. 'Good God! *You're* Mrs Petrovic?'

Rhea schooled her face into a no-nonsense expression, determined not to let her undermining feelings distract her from her resolve. 'I'm afraid so,' she said crisply. 'And you're Mr Chase, I presume.'

The frown resettled on his face. 'I didn't recognise your voice,' he said, his tone suggesting that this surprised him. Rhea found this lack of recognition perfectly reasonable, since their conversation on the phone had hardly been a calm one.

'I didn't recognise your voice either,' she countered archly.

He frowned at her brusque manner before shaking his head, then sighing. 'Sorry if I was rude on the phone. My only excuse is shock. Laura has been . . .' his lips pulled back into a sardonic grimace '. . . dare I say . . . difficult?'

Rhea bristled at his lack of sensitivity for the child. 'Children are often difficult, Mr Chase,' she pointed out. 'But packing them off to boarding school won't really fix anything. You might solve an immediate problem, but you'll eventually gain a lot more.'

She saw the flash of annoyance in his face, but to give him credit he controlled it well. 'I really think, Mrs Petrovic,' he said coolly, 'that where I send my daughter to school is hardly your business. Neither should Laura have confided family matters to a stranger. Now if you'll get her, please . . .'

He fixed steely eyes upon her, but Rhea stood her ground. Later she would marvel at her audacity. 'No,

Mr Chase, I will not.' Her chin rose, her expression matching his for fierce dignity. 'Not until I've had my say. I promised Laura I'd speak to you on her behalf.'

The grey eyes widened, then narrowed. 'That was presumptuous of you.' His voice would have frozen an entire boardroom of directors.

But it only hardened Rhea's resolution. 'I'm sorry if you're offended, but my main concern is Laura's happiness.'

'Really?' His tone and expression were coldly dry. 'That surprises me. How long have you known my daughter? An hour at most. Mrs King assures me Laura was in her room at four. And yet you tell me you're concerned for her happiness. Forgive me if I'm somewhat sceptical.'

'All right.'

'All right what?' he snapped.

'All right, I'll forgive you,' she returned with a poker face.

He was totally taken aback by her attitude. Clearly he was not used to being mocked—or challenged. Rhea realised with a measure of surprise that she was enjoying doing both. Somehow it soothed that part of her that still wanted him, despite knowing now what sort of man he was.

'It's callous of you,' she went on boldly, 'to send Laura to boarding school so soon after her mother's death, particularly when her mother promised her she would never do such a thing.'

'Good God, how on earth did you pry these private and personal details from my daughter in such a small space of time? She's been living with me now for four months and I've hardly been able to get two words out of her!'

Rhea digested this information with astonishment. She'd assumed that he had been living with Laura's mother in a *de facto* relationship. Clearly they hadn't been living together at all! 'Well, I'm hardly to blame for that, am I?' she retorted with a degree of fluster. 'Perhaps if you spent some time really listening to her . . .'

'How can I listen when she never says anything?' he argued in obvious frustration. 'God knows I've tried to gain her confidence!'

Rhea recalled how frustrated Laura had made her feel with her mutinous silence, but she blocked out any inclination to feel sympathy for the man. If he was in a difficult situation then it was his fault, wasn't it? Where had he been all his daughter's life, anyway?

'When exactly did Laura's mother pass away?' she asked.

'Last September,' he sighed.

It had been early October when Rhea had seen him kissing the blonde at the airport. 'I see,' she muttered, giving him a look of disgust.

'I doubt you do see, dear lady,' he bit out. 'Neither would you appreciate how difficult it is for a bachelor to suddenly have a child thrust upon him. I've done my best, believe me. Laura just won't co-operate!'

'All the more reason why she should stay with you now,' she advised strongly. 'You obviously need more time together. I know how my daughter would feel if I sent her away. Laura clearly thinks you want to get rid of her, that she's in the way.'

'Not true!' he denied hotly. 'I love the child. I didn't realise how much till I thought something had happened to her today . . .'

Rhea felt a reluctant empathy with him, recalling the fear and panic she had felt when Emily's school bus had been horribly late one afternoon.

'But Laura has to go to school somewhere,' he was saying. 'Have you seen that atrocity they call a school up the road? It's a relic of the last century!'

Rhea saw red. '*My* daughter goes to that relic, Mr Chase. And I'll have you know it's an excellent establishment! *Teachers* make a school, not the building, and Bangaloo Creek Primary has the best staff of teachers in the world!'

He had the grace to look apologetic. 'I didn't mean to give offence . . .'

'No? Maybe you didn't, but you didn't stop to think whether you would either. Your sort never does.'

The grey eyes dilated dangerously and he drew himself up stiff and straight. 'And what do you mean by that remark?'

Rhea's cheeks grew hot. She had gone too far and she knew it.

'Nothing, I . . . I . . .'

He grabbed her elbow and she froze.

'Tell me what you mean by *my* sort?' he demanded harshly.

She stared down at the fingers gripping her flesh and added 'violent' to his already long list of faults. Wrenching her arm away, she lifted flashing eyes.

'The sort,' she burst out, 'who wants all the pleasures of the bedroom and none of the responsibilities!'

He was staring at her as though she were mad.

And she was. Mad that she had not been able to make things right for Laura. Mad for letting the situation get totally out of hand. Mad that even a passing touch from this man could send an electric thrill charging through her body. Mad, mad, mad!

And now that her outburst was over Rhea was overwhelmed by a deep shame. How could she be so outspoken, so disgustingly rude? She groaned. 'Oh, Mr Chase, I . . . I'm so sorry. What I said . . . I didn't mean it. I . . . I don't even know you. I'm so terribly sorry.'

He remained silent, but he was looking at her closely, his expression disturbingly intense. When a small smile tugged at the corners of his mouth Rhea rocked back with astonishment. 'All right,' he said with a hint of dry amusement.

'All right?' she repeated blankly.

'All right, I forgive you,' he said, the amusement definite now in his eyes. Rhea could only stare at him as she tried desperately to get a grip on the situation. And herself.

'I must say you make a good avenging angel, Mrs Petrovic. And there may be a grain of truth in what you said.' His eyes danced wickedly. 'But only a grain. I *do* try not to deliberately hurt anyone, particularly beautiful women.'

Warmth and charisma rolled form him in waves, threatening to engulf her in their tidal force. She reacted instinctively with a cool look, but it was more a survival tactic than any form of rebuke.

He frowned, pressing his well-shaped lips into a thin

line, reminding Rhea that most women would respond eagerly to his compliments. But this knowledge only made her all the more determined not to. After all, he believed she was a married woman and so he should not be flirting with her.

Or didn't he care if she were married?

Rhea was distressed that she didn't find that thought as off-putting as she should have.

'So . . .' he breathed in deeply, then exhaled '. . .the local school has your recommendation?' His whole manner was now totally detached, almost cold.

'It does,' she murmured.

'How do I go about enrolment?' he asked brusquely.

'You just . . . just show up on Wednesday morning with Laura and see the school secretary. She'll be able to help you with everything.'

'Uniforms too?'

Rhea resisted the urge to offer him a couple of the ones Emily had outgrown. People like Stephen Chase didn't dress their daughters in hand-me-down uniforms. 'You can buy them at the Grace Brothers store in Liverpool.'

'And how old is your daughter, Mrs Petrovic?'

'Ten. She'll be eleven in April.'

'Then she'll be in the same class as Laura. She turns eleven in May.'

'Laura's *ten*?' Rhea could not hide her astonishment.

'I know—she's small for her age. Her mother was only tiny, five feet one at the most . . .'

Rhea's mind clicked over. The young woman she had seen him with in the coffee lounge could hardly qualify as tiny.

'But she's shy. For the last two years she hasn't gone to school. She travelled a lot with her mother and had a private tutor. I'm told she's bright, though.'

'How exactly did Laura's mother die?' Rhea couldn't resist asking.

'A type of food poisoning. Botulism.'

She watched his face as he spoke. It was grim, but there was no pain. Definitely no pain. Whatever his relationship had been with Laura's mother, he had not loved her. 'I gather you weren't living together at the time,' she remarked, an edge of reproach in the words.

His look carried a weary exasperation. 'No, I wasn't living with Naomi when she died. Or at any other time. *Her* choice, not mine, I can assure you. There was a time when I would have married her like a shot if she'd wanted me to.'

Rhea found that hard to swallow. She couldn't imagine that a woman who had had this man's child would pass up the chance of marrying him. Unless, of course, he had already proved himself a faithless lover . . .

'What about grandparents?' Rhea went on. 'If you're finding Laura such a problem, wouldn't she better off with them?'

His jaw clenched visibly, then relaxed. 'Naomi's parents are dead,' he explained patiently. 'As far as mine are concerned, they have offered to have Laura sometimes. But they're elderly and have already raised a large family. Besides which they would be appalled with me—as I would be with myself—if I didn't accept the responsibility of my daughter. Look, Mrs Petrovic, I realise that my bachelor status doesn't find favour with you, and that you believe I'm somehow unfit to raise a child, but I hardly think you can judge the situation on such a short acquaintance, do you?'

Against her will Rhea was impressed by the sentiments expressed in his speech. He sounded as if he genuinely wanted to do his best for Laura. And at least he came from a solid family background. Not only that, he was right: she was being judgemental.

'I'm sorry,' she said with genuine apology. 'I didn't mean to imply that you were in any way a bad parent. Laura is better off with her father than anyone else—that's why I felt so strongly about you sending her away. She needs you with her, Mr Chase. She needs your emotional support, your company, your love. She——'

She broke off when she became aware that she was speaking quite passionately, and that those penetrating grey eyes were riveted to the movements of her mouth.

His eyes lifted to lock on to hers. 'Go on,' he said.

Rhea gave a nervous laugh. 'I think I was getting a bit carried away!'

'Not at all. You're a woman of rare conviction. And to be truthful I probably needed a lecture about Laura. I've been listening to too many other people's opinions on what I should be doing with her.'

He smiled at Rhea, swamping her once again with the full force of his charm. It caught her off guard and she reacted instinctively, her mouth tightening with disapproval. And fear.

A slight sigh revealed that he had noticed her reaction. He looked away, his right hand lifting to run distractedly through his hair, disrupting its 'not a wave

out of place' order. When a lock fell across his forehead
it evoked a vulnerability at odds with the mature
strength of his features. For the first time Rhea
wondered how old he was. In his thirties, she guessed.
Possibly thirty-five or -six.

'So . . .' his eyes swung back to face her '. . . a small
school should suit Laura very well, then, shouldn't it?'

'Yes,' she agreed, her face less tense now. Ridiculous
to think his smile had been a deliberately seductive
gesture, that he was going to make a serious play for
her. This man would throw smiles at women like the
sower threw seeds, hoping that some fell on fertile
ground. Little did he know that with Rhea the seed had
already germinated.

'Not to mention a ready-made friend in class,' he
added, smiling at her again. But it wasn't the same sort
of smile this time. There was no accompanying flash
from deep within his eyes. 'You'll have to bring your
daughter around sometimes so she and Laura can play
together.'

Not on your nelly! Rhea decided. To see Laura's
father on a regular basis—even as a neighbour—was
out of the question. Talk about asking for trouble . . .
'We'll see,' she said non-committally. 'Don't you think
we should go and tell Laura the good news?'

Rhea turned and walked briskly towards the house,
Stephen Chase falling into step at her shoulder.

'You have a nice neat little place here, Mrs Petrovic,'
he said, eyes sweeping around.

Rhea glanced first at the simple but pretty garden
beds, then over at the home-made kennel, the cheaply
fenced paddocks, the small cottage, remembering quite

clearly the first time Milan had shown her the place. He had been so proud. A European migrant whose whole family had been killed in a civil uprising, he had arrived in Australia without a cent, and no qualifications. He had been an intelligent man, but times had been hard, unemployment high. The only work he had been able to find was as a contract cleaner, working long hours to save the deposit for his dream property.

Of course he would have preferred a real farm—hundreds of acres, not just five—but he had needed to live close enough to Sydney for work. He had used to promise that one day he would build a bigger, better home for them.

But that day had never come. He had been drowned in a rough sea off Kiama, trying to save a fisherman who had been swept off the rocks by a freak wave.

A wretched guilt claimed Rhea as she thought of her dead husband. He had loved her so much. And she had loved him, loved his quiet strength, his devoted sense of duty, his total commitment to his family. And yet she had not been able to give him what most men would expect from their wives.

The memory of her honeymoon came back to haunt her. At first there had been pain, too much pain. But then later, when things should have improved, there had been nothing. Milan had told her not to worry about it, that some women were just made that way. Rhea had often wondered if he minded. Certainly her lack of response had not deterred him from taking his conjugal rights, though she had often wondered why he bothered when she lay beneath him so unmoved.

It upset her to think that the man walking next to her

stirred her more with a smile than Milan had with the entire act of love.

'Do you and your husband only have the one child?'

They had reached the side door, with Stephen Chase at Rhea's shoulder. Her hand had been moving forward to grasp the knob when he threw the question at her. She froze, knowing the moment had come to enlighten him about Milan's death.

Her hand dropped back to her side and, biting her lip in agitation, she began to turn.

But she had not realised he was so close to her. As she turned she brushed against his chest, and, while he stepped back, he was still overpoweringly near. His superior male height loomed over her own five feet six, bringing a hot awareness to her body. Her cheeks pinked. Her skin prickled.

She grew even more disturbed when his left hand slid up the door-frame, the action pulling his jacket apart so that she was confronted by an impressively wide chest. He was leaning slightly forward as well, so that it would have been so easy for her to slide her hands up over that pristine shirt, to wind her arms around his muscular neck, to gently pull the gorgeous mouth down to . . .

Her eyes widened for a moment as she fought to squash her rampant fantasies, making her look unmistakably alarmed. His hand dropped from the door-frame as though stung by an electric shock. He drew himself up straight and took a further step backwards.

Shame swamped Rhea as she realised he had thought her frightened of his nearness. Her eyes dropped disconcertingly to the ground. Dear God, if only he knew!

The ensuing silence crackled with tension till Rhea pulled herself together enough to answer his question. 'Yes,' she said, lifting still panicky eyes, 'there's only Emily.' Then she wrenched open the screen door and fled inside, followed by her unwanted visitor.

'Please . . . sit down,' she offered briskly, standing well away from him, her backside hard against the sink, her hands clutching the counter on either side.

He pulled out one of the chairs that surrounded the round laminex table and sat down. Rhea thought he looked like a fish out of water in the old-fashioned kitchen, with its chipped blue cupboards and cheap vinyl floor, and while she wasn't ashamed of her home she couldn't help an inexplicable wave of depression—and an accompanying dismay.

She noticed that he was watching her closely, and her stomach churned.

'Is your husband away?' he asked unexpectedly.

Rhea grew even more flustered. 'Why . . . why do you ask that?'

He shrugged. 'You seem agitated. It occurred to me that he might not like a strange man being in the house when he's away.'

Rhea's head whirled. Now was the time to tell him quite clearly that she was a widow, to rectify his assumptions. Yet panic at what this announcement could produce made her hesitate. She was afraid she wouldn't be able to resist him if he did make a play for her. And he certainly might, once he was told the truth. He had already shown that he found her attractive.

'Yes . . . yes, he's away,' she said hurriedly, then gave

a nervous laugh. 'And you're hardly a stranger any more, Mr Chase. You're Laura's father, as well as a neighbour.'

She hoped that if his communication with Laura was as bad as he said, he might never find out the truth. After all, Stephen Chase was not the sort of father to go to school functions, or gossip down at the local club.

'I'll get your daughter for you,' she added, and hurried from the room.

Rhea's patience was tried to the limit when Laura refused at first to come with her. It was only after the girl had been assured several times of not being sent to boarding school that she made a reluctant appearance in the kitchen. Even so, the child was still nervous in her father's presence, shrinking into Rhea's skirt at his, 'Come along now, Laura. I think we've taken up enough of Mrs Petrovic's time and hospitality, don't you?'

It wasn't until Emily said, 'I'll see you on Wednesday,' that the girl let go Rhea's hand and did as her father asked.

Both Rhea and Emily walked with them to the car, but not a word passed between any of them. Even the dogs were unusually quiet. Rhea grew conscious of a tightness in her chest as she watched Stephen Chase see his daughter seated and the safety belt properly adjusted. She couldn't seem to take her eyes off his unconscious grace of movement and found she was holding her breath, as if counting the seconds till he would be safely out of sight.

He closed the passenger door and strode round to the driver's side near where Emily and Rhea were standing. He hesitated in front of her and for a ghastly moment she thought he was going to bend forward and kiss her on the cheek. Instead he murmured, 'Thank you,' and held out his hand.

'Glad to be of help,' she said with a stiff smile, and slowly lifted her own hand from her side. His fingers closed, strong and warm around hers, sending a tremor up her arm and right down to her toes. She froze, terrified that he might be aware of her reaction. But he appeared unperturbed, already dropping her hand and turning away.

Once settled behind the wheel he glanced up at her through the windscreen. It was an odd look, both hard and long, but it still affected her deeply. A timely warning for keeping to her deception, she thought ruefully.

When he finally reversed out and drove away, she was flooded with relief, dragging in a deep ragged breath.

Emily gave her a curious look. 'Did you have a fight with Laura's father?' she asked.

'Not really,' came Rhea's careful reply. 'He was open to reason once he realised how unhappy his daughter was.'

'He sure is good-looking, isn't he, Mum?'

Rhea's heart skipped a beat. 'Do you think so?' she managed with superb indifference. 'I didn't really notice.'

CHAPTER FOUR

RHEA kept herself even busier from that day on. Every morning she would rise early and have all her housework done before eight, then retire to the living-room, which served as her workshop. There she would put some music on her portable cassette—mostly soundtracks from her favourite musicals—and hum along while she worked.

Her coming autumn range was far more extensive than anything she had attempted before, for reasons of finance more than creative compulsion. The annual rates had come in, and there'd been a hefty rise. So, as well as the matching jumpers, scarves and berets, she was attempting some glamorous evening tops and shawls.

Most were made of mohair from her own fleeces, carefully spun and dyed the way she liked, with natural pigments, but sometimes she added shop-bought fibres, such as cotton or silk, if she wanted a special effect. All were handmade, either knitted or crocheted, depending on the pattern. And all were one-off articles, Rhea never repeating a style and colour combination.

With less than a month to go before delivery date, she was working every spare moment. And if that had the added benefit of keeping her mind off a certain person, she wasn't about to complain.

Emily returned to school on the Wednesday—blessedly catching the bus to and fro—and, while she did rave on every afternoon about what good friends she and Laura were becoming, no mention was made of the 'good-looking' father.

Which was just as well, Rhea thought as she rose on the following Saturday morning after a particularly restless night. Though she suspected it was only a matter of time before Emily started begging to go over to Laura's place to see the pony. In fact, her daughter had already dropped a couple of hints the previous evening.

Peeping through the curtains, Rhea was relieved to see that it was beginning to drizzle. It meant fresh grass for the goats as well as the perfect excuse to veto any suggestion of 'visiting'. She had a sinking feeling, however, that she was only delaying the inevitable. One day she would have to face Stephen Chase again. And one day he would probably find out she had misled him about her married state.

But not today, she decided as she dragged on her favourite old robe and padded out to the kitchen to make herself a cup of coffee. She yawned and reached for the kettle. Thank the Lord she wasn't playing the organ at any function that afternoon! Terrible day for a wedding anyway, she thought, yawning again.

'Is it time to get up, Mum?' came a sleepy voice from behind her.

Rhea turned. 'Not yet, love. It's Saturday, remember?'

'Oh . . . I forgot.' Whereupon Emily turned and went back to bed.

An hour later Rhea was hard at work. One garment, a scarlet evening sweater with dolman sleeves and a scooped neckline, was giving her trouble. One side wasn't quite matching the other, and, even though

Rhea's eye for shape and size was usually faultless, something had gone wrong this time.

Her hand reached down beside her chair to where she always dropped her tape-measure, but her fingers encountered a bare mat. She frowned and peered over the large arm of the chair. No tape-measure. She glanced around, knowing that it was somewhere not far away — she had used it yesterday—but still no tape-measure. She stood up and walked around, searching, picking up things.

In the end she gave up, deciding that Emily's ruler would do for the time being. She strode out into the kitchen and over to the corner behind the door, where her daughter always dropped her school-bag. It had a large zipper running across the top with a koala-shaped key-ring attached for easy undoing. When she bent over and slid the key-ring across, the two sides fell open, exposing the contents.

Rhea stared, then bent further to pick up three brown paper bags. Puzzled, she opened them. Yes . . . just as she'd thought. Emily's school lunches, untouched and uneaten.

Frowning, she put them on the kitchen table and moved slowly towards her daughter's bedroom. For a moment she hesitated in the hallway, not sure how to handle the problem. She wasn't exactly angry, but she wasn't calm either. And she knew she couldn't wait till Emily got up before tackling her about the lunches.

She opened the bedroom door and walked over to shake her daughter's shoulder. 'Emily, I need to talk to you.'

Emily blinked and yawned, then pulled herself

upright, frowning. 'What's up?'

Rhea sat down on the edge of the bed, a no-nonsense expression on her face. She had decided on the direct approach. 'Why didn't you eat your lunches at school this week?' she asked abruptly. 'I went to your bag to borrow your ruler and I found all three of them, untouched.'

There was no doubt about it—Emily looked guilty.

'You weren't sick, were you?' Rhea persisted.

'No . . .'

'Then what did you eat? Did someone else share their lunch with you?'

'Sort of . . .' faltered Emily.

'What do you mean—sort of?'

'Well, Laura had money left over and . . . well . . .'

Rhea stiffened. 'And well what?'

'Well, she orders her lunch every day from the school canteen and she sort of bought me stuff from there too.'

'Such as what?' asked Rhea through gritted teeth.

Emily was looking very uncomfortable. 'You know . . . crisps and lollies and stuff.'

'And what, pray tell, did you intend doing with your lunches? Were they to stay in your bag till they grew penicillin?' Rhea's voice had risen to a shriek.

Emily bit her bottom lip. 'I was going to give them to the goats today,' she whispered.

'Were you, now?' Rhea glared at her daughter.

'Yes . . .' The whisper was barely a squeak.

The frightened quality in her daughter's voice suddenly got through to Rhea and she felt terrible. Emily had been wrong in what she had done, but as a mother, she wasn't behaving so well either, ranting and raving like a fishwife.

'I'm sorry, Mum,' Emily sobbed, tears spilling over.

Rhea pulled her daughter into a fierce hug. 'I'm sorry too, love,' she soothed, stroking Emily's long hair. 'I shouldn't have shouted at you. You're not entirely to blame—not many people can resist having goodies bought for them. I understand, really I do.'

She drew back from the embrace and gave Emily an understanding look. 'But you must know that I try to pack you a sensible lunch, with proper nutrition. Crisps and lollies are all very well as an occasional treat, but not as a substitute for lunch. Do you understand?'

'I suppose so.' Emily didn't look entirely convinced.

'I give you two dollars a week,' Rhea reminded her. 'You can spend that on crisps and the like, *after* you've eaten your lunch.'

'Laura gets five dollars a day,' Emily said resentfully.

'Oh, surely not!'

'Yes, she does. And that's just for her lunch. She's got other money as well.'

Rhea stood up. She was aware of a growing anger deep inside her, an anger directed at one person in particular. Damned Stephen Chase! Did he have to ruin everything? Even her relationship with her daughter?

'You must realise, Emily,' she said strongly, 'that such a sum is a ridiculous amount of money to give a child. Her father's a fool!'

Emily pouted. 'Laura says he's real nice now. She likes him a lot.'

How typical of the man! Rhea fumed. Using his money to buy love!

She glared at her daughter's rebellious expression

and decided she was speaking to the wrong person. If she was to stop this situation from continuing she would have to deal with the source of the problem.

Heat raced into her cheeks at the prospect of another face-to-face confrontation with Stephen Chase till she remembered the phone. Anything she had to say to him could be handled quite well that way. There was no need to put up with his disturbing physical presence.

She stopped in the doorway and glanced back at her daughter. 'I want your promise, Emily, that you will always eat the lunch I give you. Unless you're sick, of course. If I find you disobey me in this, you won't even get your two dollars. Do I make myself clear?'

'Yes, Mum.' Emily sank back under the covers.

'Good!'

Rhea marched down the hallway, back into the kitchen and over to the counter. She flicked open her notebook to the page where the number was, then dialled before she could think better of it.

A woman answered on the second ring. 'Mr Chase's residence. Mrs King speaking.'

'I would like to speak to Mr Chase, please,' Rhea said nervously. Her heart was going at fifty to the dozen, fuelled she believed by her indignation.

'Oh, I think he's just left . . . Wait . . . No, I might be able to catch him . . .'

Rhea was left dangling for some minutes. It did nothing to improve her state of nerves—or her temper. Suddenly she heard Mrs King saying in the background, 'I don't know who it is, Mr Chase. A lady . . . She didn't give her name.'

'Did it sound like Madeline?'

'Oh no, Mr Chase, not at all.'

Rhea bristled. No doubt Madeline was his current lady-love, all glamour and polish, complete with a posh accent, not like Rhea's good old Australian drawl. Probably the sophisticated blonde at the airport. Or maybe a new one. He seemed to go for blondes!

There was a rustling sound and then the voice she was dreading. 'Stephen Chase speaking.'

Rhea took a deep breath. 'Mr Chase, I'm sorry to bother you, but I have this problem with Emily and I—'

'Mrs Petrovic?' he interrupted in sharp puzzlement. 'That is you, isn't it?'

Rhea almost died of mortification. Oh God, here she was trying to play the firm negotiator and she had forgotten to tell him who was calling.

'Yes, it's me.' Her voice sounded as deflated as her pride.

'You have a problem with your daughter? Something I can help you with?'

'No, I . . . I mean yes . . .' Rhea was hopelessly rattled. 'I was hoping you could,' she finished lamely.

'I'll do what I can. But I think perhaps you're the expert with children, not me. The change in Laura since going to that little school of yours is remarkable. I never used to be able to get her to talk. Now my only problem seems to be shutting her up,' he chuckled. 'But I'm getting off the point here, aren't I? What's Emily been up to?'

'It concerns Laura as well,' Rhea choked out.

'Oh?' There was a frown in the word.

Rhea swallowed.

'You sound upset, Mrs Petrovic,' he went on, his tone now one of sincere concern. It totally squashed any anger in her. 'I hope it's nothing serious. Would you like me to come over?'

'No!' Panic—absolute panic.

'Then can you tell me what it is? Has Laura said something . . . done something to upset Emily? I thought they'd become great mates. Laura talks of no one else.'

'It isn't really Laura's fault, Mr Chase,' Rhea blurted out.

'You certainly have me puzzled. Could you be more specific?'

'It . . . it's the lunch money you give her, you see,' she said haltingly. 'She's been . . . buying Emily sweets from the school canteen and Emily hasn't been eating her lunch.'

He laughed. 'Is that all? My goodness, you had me going there for a while! I was imagining all sorts of things.'

His amusement revitalised a surge of indignation. 'It's not a laughing matter, Mr Chase. I happen to take my daughter's eating habits very seriously. A child her age needs proper nutrition. I thought you would be similarly concerned about Laura's diet. Of course, I may have been mistaken about your intentions the other day. I got the impression you wanted to be a good father, despite your late start!'

She heard him sigh. 'I do want to be a good father, Mrs Petrovic. And I'm sure I can rely upon you to set me right whenever I stray from the straight and narrow of correct parenting.' There was no denying the weary frustration in his words.

Rhea felt guilty now. Every time she talked to the man she seemed to run off at the mouth. Nerves, she realised. But that was no real excuse. 'I'm sorry, I don't mean to be critical,' she tried to back-pedal.

'Of course not.'

'I . . . I only have the children's best interests at heart.'

'Naturally.'

'I mean . . . You couldn't be expected to know about the prices at the school canteen. You probably haven't got a list.'

'I'm so glad you're beginning to understand.' His words held a heavy-handed patience.

Rhea fell silent. She felt terribly small. 'I'm sorry to have bothered you,' she managed at last.

'Don't hang up!' he ordered.

'W—what?'

'I'll be in terrible trouble if I let you get away now that I have you on the phone. Laura's been asking me to ring you to invite Emily over. However, I wasn't sure if such an invitation would be welcome. I'm aware you don't exactly approve of me . . .'

He stopped then, obviously waiting for Rhea to make some retaliatory comment, but she could think of nothing to say. Besides, she wasn't sure her voice would work even if she could.

There was another deep sigh. 'Look, Mrs Petrovic, I know I got off on the wrong foot with you, accusing you of being a kidnapper. And I gather you aren't too impressed that Laura's mother and I were never married, but believe me, that was not my fault. Would it make any difference if I explained what happened there?'

'Oh, no, you don't have to,' Rhea blustered, through secretly dying to know.

'I realise that, but I want to. Believe it or not, your good opinion is important to me. We're members of the same small community, and our daughters seem intent on being firm friends. I would hate for you to refuse permission for Emily to come over sometimes because you think her father is some sort of rotter.'

'Oh, but I don't think——'

'Oh, but you do, dear lady. You definitely do.'

Embarrassment held her silent.

'I appreciate how it must look to outsiders,' he went on. 'The truth is that Naomi—Laura's mother—never told me that she was pregnant. She was a good deal older than the twenty-one I was at the time . . .'

Rhea frowned. Twenty-*one*? But that would mean he was only thirty-one or two at the most now. And yet he looked older. Hard living, perhaps?

'It was the typical case of the young man infatuated with an older woman. As I said before, I would have married her despite our age difference, but that was not Naomi's plan. She wanted only one thing, it seems—a baby. You know the situation. A career woman finds herself in her thirties, wants a child, but not a husband. I happened to be the bunny she chose to be the father . . .'

Rhea could visualise why. At twenty-one Stephen must have been the most gorgeous, virile . . .

'. . . but I knew nothing of Laura till after Naomi died last year in Paris. There was a letter addressed to me in her papers. You can imagine my surprise to find I had a ten-year-old daughter. I——' He broke off, irritated perhaps that he was justifying his actions to her, a mere neighbour. 'Hell, give me some credit, Mrs Petrovic, it hasn't been easy, and I am doing my best!'

'You've acted very responsibly, Mr Chase,' Rhea admitted. 'Considering. I mean . . . oh, dear, I've done it again, haven't I?'

His chuckle was low and warm. 'What say we wipe the slate clean and start again, eh? At least for the sake of the children,' he added, wry humour to the fore.

It brought a reluctant smile to Rhea's lips. 'All right,' she murmured. To say anything else would have been the height of intolerance.

'And what shall I call you? Mrs Petrovic is a bit of a mouthful, isn't it?'

'My name is Rhea. Spelt R-H-E-A.'

'Rhea . . . Unusual. And I answer to Stephen. Now, let me make a suggestion, Rhea . . .'

How marvellous her name sounded on his tongue. Like a softly played arpeggio.

'Why don't you drop over later today with Emily? I know Laura's dying to show off her pony. You could bring me one of those canteen price lists and tell me what I should order for Laura, and what a suitable amount of pocket-money is. What do you say?'

Rhea hesitated. It all sounded harmless enough. Though not even the shortest visit would be harmless, considering the feelings and thoughts he always evoked in her. 'But weren't you just leaving to go somewhere?' she floundered.

'Only to the local shop to buy the papers.'

'Oh . . .' There was no reasonable excuse she could think of not to go.

And she wanted to see him. Just see him. There! She had admitted it. Even if the mere thought made her pulse go wild. Even if she didn't get a wink's sleep for a month. 'I . . . I can't make it till after lunch,' she said, her hesitancy belying what she considered an incredibly bold move.

'Fine.'

'Will two . . . two o'clock be all right?'

'Any time.'

She firmed her jaw to keep her voice steady. 'Two it will be, then, Mr Chase.'

'*Stephen*, remember?'

'Stephen.'

She hung up, his name quivering on her lips.

CHAPTER FIVE

'IT'S stopped raining!' Emily exclaimed excitedly as they drove up the road shortly before two. 'Look, the sun's coming out. Laura and I will be able to have a ride on her pony. Oh, I can't wait to get there!' She grinned at her mother. 'Are they new jeans you're wearing?'

'No.'

'I don't remember seeing them before. But I like them—they make you look young. And that yellow top is my favourite.'

Rhea gave her daughter a wry smile. 'You wouldn't be buttering me up for something, would you?'

'Gosh, no!'

'Well, before you go all gaga over Laura's pony, I want to tell you that if Dolly has more than two pups I'm going to use the money from selling them to buy you a pony of your own.'

Rhea's heart turned over at the look on Emily's face.

'Oh, Mum, do you mean it? Do you really?'

'I do indeed,' smiled Rhea.

'Oh, thank you, thank you! And I'm sure Dolly's having at least six pups. She's as big as the side of a bus!'

Rhea laughed. 'She certainly is.'

Her laughter died once she turned the van into Mountain View Road, tension invading as she battled to keep her apprehension down and her resolve up.

Rhea had decided to tell Stephen she was a widow—not because she wanted him to know she was free, but because it was stupid to keep the deception going. He was sure to find out now that he and Laura were communicating.

But it wouldn't be easy to bring the subject up, she conceded nervously. What was she to say? By the way, Stephen, I was only joking the other day when I said my husband was away. Actually he's dead . . .

Oh, God, what a mess I've got myself into! Rhea groaned silently. In more ways than one.

She lifted a hand to see if her hair was still up. She had twisted it into what she had thought was a sensible knot, but as she glanced in the rear-vision mirror she began to worry that the continuously escaping strands lent a totally wrong image. Instead of her hair looking sleek and controlled, it seemed to project an impression of enforced imprisonment, like a wild thing caged for its own protection, just waiting to spring free and wreak havoc.

Like me, came the insidious thought.

Emily didn't appear to notice her mother's distracted state. She chattered away, exclaiming over the size and grandeur of Laura's house as the van slowly chugged up the steep hill towards it.

In truth, it wasn't a mansion. But by Emily's youthful standards it probably seemed to be. 'Isn't it fantastic, Mum? Wouldn't you like to live in a house like that?'

Rhea's tense glare flicked over the two-storeyed, Tudor-style dwelling, her thoughts taking a rueful twist at her daughter's words. Yes, she conceded with a shaming truth, she would like to live in this particular house . . . for a night or two.

But she turned a gentle glance towards her daughter. 'Money isn't everything, love.'

'No, I guess not.'

Even so, Rhea had to admit that the house and its surroundings were imposing, perched as they were on top of a hill. It was hard not to compare the 'no expense spared' quality with their own simple lifestyle.

Proper cement bridges spanned the entrance and exit to a wide, semi-circular approach that was bordered in stained logs and filled with tiny river pebbles. A brick wall extended for several metres on either side of the house and blocked any view of the back yard, but Rhea had no doubt that there would be the obligatory swimming-pool and tennis-court. Men like Stephen Chase never wanted for anything.

It was a sobering thought.

Rhea braked to a halt at the base of the front steps, the van shuddering with relief. Not so her nerves. They didn't improve either when the heavy cedar front door opened and an excited Laura spilled out, closely followed by her father.

Rhea opened the car door and virtually leapt from behind the wheel, afraid that he would do something chivalrous like help her out. Instinct told her that she was relatively safe, if she kept him at a distance.

'I do so like punctual people,' he beamed, striding down the steps towards her, looking disgustingly handsome in casual grey trousers and an open-necked blue and white striped shirt. With a kind of sick fascination, her eyes were drawn to the exposed V of chest where fine black hairs swirled into soft curls, curls that she knew would feel soft under her fingers, would . . .

Her eyes snapped up to his, appalled at how quickly her imagination ran wild whenever she was near this man.

He frowned at her, and it took Rhea some moments

to realise it was because her own features had twisted with self-recrimination. It took a deliberate effort to relax her mouth into a smile.

'Come on, Em,' Laura was saying in the background, 'let's go down and see Mimi. Now that it's stopped raining we can saddle her up and go for a ride.'

Already they were beginning to run off.

'You be careful, Emily!' Rhea shouted after the fast-disappearing girls. 'No mad galloping, and I'll pick you up at five, OK?'

Emily turned and waved. 'OK!'

'Pick up?' Stephen repeated slowly. 'I thought you were going to stay.'

Rhea swallowed. 'I am, but . . . but not for three hours. I have work to do at home.'

'Has your husband returned?'

Now was the moment to tell him. There is no husband . . . But suddenly a million unnamed fears gripped her, and the words just wouldn't come.

'N-no—no, he hasn't. I use my home as a workshop, making specialised knitwear.'

She felt oddly gratified by his obvious surprise.

'I have a few angora goats,' she went on, suddenly impelled by an irrational and unnecessary need to impress him. 'I spin and dye the mohair myself, then fashion original garments for sale in boutiques.'

His hand had somehow found her elbow and he was directing her towards his front door. Rhea was too stunned to pull away. His fingertips seemed to be burning their brand into her skin, propelling her along a previously unknown path. So this is what it feels like to be overwhelmed by desire, she thought dazedly.

Helpless, breathless, reckless . . .

'How fascinating,' Stephen was saying. 'When do you find the time?'

'Time?' she repeated blankly.

'You look after a husband and child, as well as dogs and goats, not to mention playing the organ. Now you tell me you make clothes as well. You must get very tired.'

'Sometimes,' she choked out, hating herself for letting the misconception continue.

'All the more reason why you should take this opportunity to put your feet up for a while. Besides, you promised to explain to me all about the canteen.'

She ground to a halt at the front door, her blush deep and instant. 'Oh dear, I forgot the price list . . .' Which wasn't surprising. Her mind had been in a whirl since the moment she had agreed to his invitation.

'Never mind. Another time will do.' His smile bestowed understanding—and potent charm. 'Would you like a cool drink, or a cup of coffee?' he asked as he ushered her inside.

It was indeed a beautiful house—though Rhea was hardly in the frame of mind for noticing details of décor. She vaguely recalled a deep-piled mint-green carpet running throughout the foyer and hall, then a very modern grey and white kitchen. Her host seated her in the room beyond the kitchen, a family room she supposed one would call it, with wide windows, a parquet floor and expensive leather furniture in a warm ochre colour.

Rhea was glad to be able to occupy her mind watching Emily and Laura in the distant paddock. Not with total success, however. Agreeing to a cup of coffee was a far cry from agreeing to an affair, but somehow it felt the same. She couldn't get out of her mind that she was the fly to Stephen's spider, and that he was just waiting patiently, playing the gentleman before making his move. And then what would happen?

'Milk and sugar?' he called from the kitchen.

'Milk, no sugar,' came her shaky reply.

She turned her head when she heard him come into the room, her gaze travelling over his well-proportioned body as he walked towards her, two coffee mugs in his hand. Rhea was shocked at the intense charge she received just watching him move—shocked and ashamed. She tore her eyes away, wishing with all her heart that she hadn't been so weak as to come.

'I forgot to ask you if you preferred decaffeinated,' he said as he placed the mugs on the coffee table in front of her chair. 'Most people don't, but I have the feeling you might be one of those health-food addicts . . .'

Her eyes flew to his, a ready retort coming to her lips. But he was smiling so charmingly at her that she found herself smiling back. 'You shouldn't tease, you know,' came her soft rebuke.

'Would I do that?' Stephen laughed as he sat down in the chair opposite, and Rhea thought how laughter changed his face from handsome to devastating. Their eyes met momentarily, his grey ones sweeping over her face and body with an unexpectedly frank appreciation. I find you desirable, they seemed to be saying. I'd like to make love to you . . .

Her heart stopped. She looked away, then back. His expression now was quite closed and she wondered if she had imagined that brief message. Her imagination was certainly working overtime lately!

She stared grimly down into the coffee mug.

When he leant forward and lightly touched her fingers, her hand froze, her head jerking up to look at him. 'Why the frown, Rhea? Have I said something to offend you? I was only joking about the health foods, you know.'

A depressing awareness that her inner panic was escalating brought Rhea up with a jolt. Pride insisted that she get herself under control.

'Of course you were,' she said with a quick bright smile.

He gave her a look that showed he wasn't quite sure how to take her.

'You must tell me,' she went on as she picked up her coffee mug, 'why you chose to build your home way out here.' It was merely something to say, though the question had probably lurked in her subconscious for quite a while.

He shrugged. 'Convenience, I suppose.'

'Convenience?' She gave a short laugh. 'I wouldn't call Bangaloo Creek in any way convenient. We have to travel miles to even go to the doctor.'

'That wasn't what I meant,' he explained. 'As soon as I found out about Laura I decided I didn't want her to grow up in the city. Too much pollution!' He slanted Rhea a meaningful look. 'That should find favour with you. No, don't defend yourself, you and I both know you've been quite right in everything you said to me. I know nothing at all about fathering, but I'm a willing learner. Anyway, my problem was finding a house on a rural acreage which wasn't too far from my office in Sydney. I'd recently bought this land as an investment for my company and it seemed quicker to build a house here than find one suitable to buy.'

'It certainly went up quickly enough,' Rhea murmured thoughtfully. So he owned a company. What kind? she wondered.

'Amazing what a promised bonus to the building supervisor can do,' he added.

The thought slid into Rhea's mind that whatever Stephen Chase couldn't get through normal channels he would buy.

She glanced up at him over the rim of her mug to see him glaring irritably at her. 'You really let your feelings show on your face, do you know that? I said *bonus*, Rhea, not a bribe. It happens to be a very normal business practice, not some shifty, underhanded tactic!'

Rhea was taken aback by his outburst—and thoroughly embarrassed. She hadn't realised she was so transparent. She placed the mug carefully down on the glass table. 'I'm sorry . . .'

He sighed. 'You don't have to apologise, Rhea. However, I wish I knew why you're so quick to judge me.'

A wave of heat swept up her neck.

'Is it because of the way I spoke to you at the wedding?' he asked softly. 'Did you think I was trying to pick you up?'

She shook her head in wide-eyed denial.

His sad smile threw her. 'I think it is, Rhea. And do you know what? I was . . .'

Rhea's eyes grew wider.

'I wasn't to know you were married,' he elaborated. 'Not only that, I'm quite experienced at picking up signals from women. And I picked up definite signals from you that day.'

'That's not true,' she rasped. 'I . . . I hardly spoke to you. I . . .' Her voiced trailed away, the guilty heat in her face much more telling than any verbal protest. A strangled, shamed sound fluttered from her throat.

The silence in the room was electric.

'And I like you too,' said Stephen at last. 'Much too much.'

Her groan was one of total confusion and panic, her eyes swinging away, then returning to his in a type of pained pleading.

'God, woman, don't look at me like that! I'm not about to jump on you.'

Rhea forced herself up on to shaking legs.

He leapt to his feet. 'Don't you dare leave!'

'I . . . I have to . . .' She began to move towards the door, but he stopped her, curving firm hands over her slender shoulders.

'No, you don't *have* to. You're an adult, with free will, Rhea Petrovic. OK, so we're attracted to each other. Admit it! I do. But you're a married woman and I'll respect that, but that doesn't mean we can't be friends, does it? Does it?' he repeated, shaking her.

Rhea was incapable of answering. She looked up into his flushed face, increasingly aware that he was staring down at her full quivering lips with a disturbing hunger. 'What is it with that husband of yours anyway?' he growled. 'Is the man mad, that he goes away and leaves you alone all the time? The fool's asking for trouble. Doesn't he realise how beautiful you are? Beautiful and sensual and desirable . . .'

He lifted his hands to cup her face, rubbing his thumbs over her cheekbones. She groaned and closed her eyes, turning her face away from his touch, but only succeeded in pressing her lips against one of his palms. When she heard the air whoosh out of his lungs her eyes flew to his. He wanted her, came the amazing thought, perhaps almost as much as she wanted him.

She battled to keep the insidious feelings from taking over her body, reminding herself of the dangers this type of man presented. Sheer common sense screamed at her to pull back, to stop him. For if she didn't, then all would be lost.

But how could she when he was looking down at her with such passion? One hand moved from her cheek to smooth across her forehead, making her shiver. The feathery fingertips then pressed her eyelids shut before following the line of her nose down to the corner of her mouth.

Rhea took a ragged breath, hoping to get some air into her starving lungs. She had ceased breathing from the moment he touched her.

'Beautiful lips,' he murmured, his words thick with arousal as his touch traced her mouth. 'Beautiful Rhea ...'

Her eyes fluttered open again to see his head slowly descending.

But then he hesitated, looking deeply into her eyes, waiting perhaps for her to resist, to protest, or shout, or do something. The future flashed into her mind with a blinding and startling clarity. Within seconds of Stephen's kissing her she would be blurting out the truth, giving him the perfect excuse to go full steam ahead. In no time she would be in his arms, then ...

Her well-ordered life would become a shambles, her hard-won independence and peace of mind a thing of the past. And it wasn't only herself who would end up being hurt. There was Emily to consider, Emily who deserved more than a mess of a mother. Rhea's only hope was hold on to whatever means she had to protect herself and her child.

She pulled back. 'No, Stephen,' she said shakily.

Stephen looked as if she had slapped him. 'But . . .'

'No . . . This is not what I want.' Was that her voice? So clear, so strong . . .

He stared at her for an eternity, clearly troubled, not at all accepting of her words. 'Rhea,' he urged, 'are you happy?'

'I'm very happy,' she said stiffly.

He shook his head. 'I find that hard to believe.' He gave her a sharp glance before shaking his head. 'And I suppose you won't even accept my friendship now, will you?'

'Stephen, I don't think that . . .'

'I promise this will never happen again,' he insisted. 'Contrary to what you think of me, I don't play around with happily married women.'

What about unhappily married ones? came the cynical thought. Rhea was not so gullible as to think he wouldn't try again, if and when he got her alone. 'I must go,' she said grimly. 'I'll come back for Emily at five.'

He sighed, closing his eyes briefly before looking at her again, his expression bleak. 'I'll see you to the door.'

Rhea made it all the way home and into her bedroom before she burst into tears. She felt shattered—totally shattered. She tried telling herself that she had done the right thing, the only thing. But somehow her heart did not agree.

Heart?

Rhea sat bolt upright. What had her heart got to do with it? It was her body she was having to fight, wasn't it? Her body and its uncharacteristic, uncontrollable desires . . .

And yet what she kept thinking about wasn't what it would feel like to have Stephen take physical possession of her. Her mind kept recalling the incredible tenderness of his touch, the gentleness. She had wanted to lose herself in his arms, not only to assuage her aching body, but to gain solace for her lonely soul. The way he had caressed her had made her feel cherished, loved . . .

Rhea jumped to her feet, angry now. It was one thing to know Stephen Chase desired her, quite another to start fantasising that he might love her. That was the stuff movies were made of. Stephen wanted her, and he wanted her unencumbered, without a husband lurking in the background. Men like him didn't change their spots. They had affairs, not relationships. They had mistresses, not wives. And she'd better never forget it!

But all the logic in the world couldn't blot out how he had made her feel in those brief, wonderful moments—far more warm, more responsive, more female than she had ever felt in her life.

Rhea shivered, admitting to herself that, if Stephen ever chose to touch her again, she could not resist a second time.

CHAPTER SIX

RHEA handed the problem of picking up Emily the only way she could bear. She asked Gavin Bicksford, the next-door neighbour's son, to do it for her, making the excuse to Mrs Bicksford about having a migraine and being unable to drive.

Needless to say she paced up and down as she awaited Emily's arrival, half expecting Stephen to ring and make some enquiry about her health. But he didn't, and for that she was grateful, though not surprised. He had sensibly decided not to pursue her further.

She had not, however, anticipated her daughter querying her behaviour.

'But you never get migraines,' Emily puzzled as soon as she got home.

Rhea didn't look up from where she had just begun peeling the potatoes for the night's meal. 'They strike some people later in life,' she muttered.

'Then shouldn't you be in bed? I can do that.'

Emily went to take the vegetable peeler out of her mother's hand, but Rhea refused. 'I'm feeling better now,' she said. 'And it helps to keep busy.'

Emily pulled out a chair at the kitchen table and sat down. 'Mr Chase seemed put out when you didn't come to pick me up,' she said. There was a short sharp silence, then Emily asked, 'Don't you like Mr Chase, Mum?'

Rhea glanced up. 'Why do you say that?'

Her daughter shrugged. 'Oh, you know . . . I can just tell.'

Rhea resumed peeling, her hand actions stiff and clumsy. 'I don't dislike him really,' she said tautly. 'But he's not my type of man.'

'Oh . . . Laura and I were hoping . . .'

Rhea's hands stilled. 'Hoping what, for heaven's sake?'

Emily looked uncomfortable. 'Nothing . . . It was Laura's idea. I mean . . .' She gave her mother a worried look, then burst out, 'Well, she was telling me how her father's just broken up with this actress he's being going out with for ages—Madeline something or other. They had an argument after he told her Laura wasn't going away to boarding school. It was her idea, it seems . . .'

So she had happened into Stephen Chase's life between bedmates, had she? It made his pursuit of someone like her more understandable.

'Anyway, Laura reckons her father didn't really love this Madeline. But she told me if he married her she would have run away again. But she said she wouldn't mind if he married you, even though she knew it could never happen because you were already married. But then I told her that no, you weren't, that my dad was dead, and she said wouldn't it be fantastic if you and her father got together!'

Emily was as breathless as Rhea by the time she finished. All Rhea could think of was that it wouldn't be long before Laura blurted out the truth about Emily's father's being dead. And then there would be hell to pay!

Emily sighed at her mother's shocked silence. 'I know you're always saying you don't want to get married again. But, Mum, that's silly! You're real pretty, and you can't be sad about Dad dying forever. I know you probably loved him a lot, but Mr Chase is real nice. He played games with us this afternoon when it started raining again. And I miss not having a dad of my own. Mum . . .?'

Tears raced into Rhea's eyes. Tears for all the lies she'd been living with for years. For as she had listened to Emily talk of her father, Rhea realised with a crippling burst of honesty that she had never loved Milan, not as a woman should love a man. She had married him as an escape from what she considered an intolerable life at home. He had been the typical father-figure, older and totally dominating, taking her young life into his hands and moulding her into what he considered a dutiful spouse should be.

Oh, yes, she had cared for him, but as an obedient daughter more than a wife, a grateful girl more than a mature woman. It was a pitiful tribute to her marriage that she much preferred her life since being widowed. That was why she had resolved never to marry again. Not so much as a noble sacrifice for Emily's sake. It was quite clear her daughter would welcome the right stepfather. No . . . she had not wanted to have to lie there in a marital bed, night after night, enduring . . . enduring . . .

But that was not the case any more, was it? She was well and truly awakened. But it wrenched at her insides to think that, having finally achieved this long-awaited womanhood, she would choose a man such as Stephen Chase. Emily was just a child. She couldn't understand that Laura's father would never marry her, would never offer anything more than a passing sexual relationship, an affair.

More tears flowed as another more devastating realisation set in. She was in danger of falling in love with this man. Crazily, madly, irrevocably . . .

'Please don't cry, Mum,' Emily sobbed, racing

around to wrap fierce arms around her mother's waist. 'I'm sorry, I shouldn't have talked about Dad dying. I'm really sorry. Please . . . I'll tell Laura never to mention it again. And I'll make sure she doesn't say anything embarrassing to her father.'

'It's all right, love,' Rhea managed on seeing her daughter's distress. 'It's not what you said, really . . . It's just this headache.'

'You should lie down for a while, Mum. Let me finish the potatoes.'

Suddenly all the energy drained out of Rhea. Her shoulders slumped and the idea of lying down was very appealing.

'I can cook the dinner,' her daughter offered. 'You go and rest.'

Rhea gave Emily a grateful smile through misty eyes and walked slowly from the kitchen. She made her way along the narrow hallway and into her tiny bedroom. A sleep would do her good, she decided as she sank down on to the edge of the crocheted quilt. You couldn't think while you were asleep. Then later, after dinner, she would get up and work.

Yes, work was always a good antidote for problems. Rhea kicked off her shoes and lay back. But sleep was slow in coming. Slow . . . And not as soothing as she had hoped.

By the following Tuesday evening Rhea was still having difficulty with the scarlet evening top. Three times she had unravelled and redone the neckline, but not to her satisfaction. She hurried back to the living-room after an early dinner, intent on giving it one final try, knowing she would not be happy to offer it for sale as it was.

She had been hard at work for over an hour when Emily popped her head into the room. 'Hey, Mum, aren't we going to the meeting up at the school? It's almost seven-thirty!'

Rhea jumped to her feet, the things in her lap scattering on to the floor. 'Oh, my goodness, I forgot!' She scooped up the mess and tossed it all on to the armchair, then hurried from the room. 'There's no time to change,' she muttered as she stuffed the minutes book into her large carryall. 'They'll just have to take me as I am, ponytail, old clothes and all. Come on, Emily, let's go.

Rhea glanced in the rear-vision mirror as she reversed out of the drive and sped up the road. 'Goodness, I look a mess!' she groaned. It was just as well that her old blue jeans and black granny top had been fresh on that morning.

'I think you look very young and pretty,' Emily insisted.

'You're a dear,' smiled Rhea, but as she swung the van into the paddock that served as a school yard, the smile died on her lips.

One of the cars already parked there was sleek and low and silver.

Her first thought was to reverse out and go straight back home. But there was a limit to how many migraines she could claim in one week. And she was the secretary of the Parents' and Citizens' Association, after all. How could they conduct the first and most important meeting of the year without her?

Of course all that wonderful reasoning didn't stop the sick nerves crowding into her stomach as she locked up the van. Who would have dreamt that Stephen would turn up at a parents' meeting?

Rhea's eyes lifted to the school, and she remembered how he had disparaged it as an old relic. Which no doubt it was . . . structurally. The barnlike building with its high-pitched iron roof and wide wooden verandas would not have won any architectural prizes, and its three classrooms weren't sufficient for the school's needs any longer, which was why there were four portable classrooms under the trees behind it.

But it was still a good school, as Rhea had defended. A happy school. And Rhea had been happy in her position of secretary of the P & C. It had brought her out of her shell, given her confidence. At least it had, up till now . . .

Her legs felt heavy as they mounted the steps on to the veranda where she stopped to give Emily a goodbye peck on the cheek. 'You behave yourself for Mrs Fraser now,' she warned. 'And keep the noise down.'

Emily hurried into the fourth-class room where Mrs Fraser, an old-age pensioner, kindly minded any children on meeting nights.

With marked reluctance Rhea walked along to the far end of the veranda, and the sixth-class room which served as their meeting place. She paused before the door and gathered every resource of inner strength she had, yet her hand still trembled as she turned the doorknob and went in.

'Sorry I'm late,' she said perfunctorily, and made her way to where she always sat, at the front, to the right of the teacher's desk. All eyes followed her, and it bothered Rhea considerably that tonight of all nights she looked as she did, but she kept her chin up and her own eyes rigidly forward.

'Don,' she murmured, nodding to the headmaster who was standing behind the teacher's desk. She sat down, extracting the minutes book and a Biro before propping her bag against the legs of her chair. Having put them on the desk she looked up, her expression admirably bland.

Several familiar faces smiled at her. She smiled back.

One face, however, was definitely not smiling.

He was sitting at a desk to the right of her, three rows back, but still close enough for her to see the unmistakable message that was glaring from those steely grey eyes.

He *knew*!

Who had told him? her mind raced. Laura? Some local? Had he perhaps started asking questions about her errant husband, only to find he didn't exist any more?

'Since we're running late,' boomed Don Gregson, 'I think we'll dispense with the reading of the minutes of the last meeting.'

He had one of those typical schoolteacher voices that carried, and tonight it seemed to cut right through Rhea's head.

'As you know, the last president of the P & C, Mrs Doreen Stonewell, has left the district, so we'll have to find ourselves a new victim—I mean volunteer . . .' He chuckled, as did several others. 'Any nominations?'

There was an ominous silence.

Rhea fiddled with the Biro and stared blankly at the floor.

'Perhaps Mr Chase will take on the job,' he suggested at last.

Rhea's eyes snapped up.

'What about it, Steve?' Don went on, a wide smile on his ruddy face.

Rhea was stunned as much by the familiarity of the headmaster's manner as the suggestion itself. It seemed to intimate that Stephen Chase was already a tried and true friend in the community, something that usually took much longer than the few short weeks he'd been living in the area. The people of Bangaloo Creek were a reserved bunch, cautious in the giving of friendship.

Her eyes shot to the object of her thoughts. He looked totally unperturbed, his long legs stretched out beside the desk, ankles crossed. He dwarfed the furniture but still didn't look awkward.

'Let's put it this way,' Stephen said with a dry laugh. 'I haven't got a clue what a Parents' Association does yet, let alone its president. Perhaps it would be better to nominate someone more familiar with the task.'

'There's nothing to it,' he was assured. 'A simple matter of chairing meetings, plus the occasional speech—child's play to the managing director of a company. Rhea here could show you the ropes, couldn't you Rhea?'

She swallowed as those assessing grey eyes swung her way. The way he arched a single dark eyebrow was decidedly cynical.

'Oh ... er ... yes, I suppose so.' She had difficulty getting the words out, so much so that her strangled tone sounded most unenthusiastic.

Out of the corner of her eye she saw a flicker of cold anger pass across Stephen's face. 'I don't think Mrs Petrovic looks too keen on the idea.'

'Ridiculous,' the headmaster vetoed forcefully. 'She'd be delighted, wouldn't you, Rhea?'

'Er ...' Rhea felt cornered for a few seconds, then annoyed. With herself, as usual. 'We can always do with some fresh blood,' she pronounced firmly, then topped it off with a dazzling smile.

It brought an immediate frown to Stephen's face—and a measure of satisfaction to her bruised self-esteem. Till he smiled back. There was something vaguely threatening hidden in that smile.

'Great!' the headmaster exclaimed heartily. 'Then I officially nominate Mr Stephen Chase for the position of President of the Bangaloo Creek P & C. Rhea? Will someone second the nomination? Good! Better note that down for the minutes. Secretary and treasurer to remain the same. That *is* all right with you, Betty, isn't it?'

Betty Waymouth, a young local mother, nodded vigorously, then slid a blatantly admiring glance over at Stephen. Rhea sighed, thinking it was just as well Betty's husband wasn't present, but took some comfort from seeing that Stephen affected all women the same way. She herself was not the exception but the rule!

'That's all settled, then,' Don continued happily. 'Steve, why don't you come up and take this seat and you can chair the meeting?'

Rhea would have had sympathy for most people being thrown in at the deep end like that, but Stephen stood up and came forward with such supreme confidence that she only felt irritation. Why couldn't he be like other people? Unsure ... hesitant ... *human*!

But no! He wasn't like other people. He certainly wasn't like any of the other men in this room, dressed as he was in an elegant business suit, the sheen on the dark grey material advertising an expensive silk blend.

Not that any of the others would look so well in it. This man had the body, the bearing to make the most of whatever he wore, be it Pierre Cardin or Levis.

Rhea realised before it became embarrassing that she was staring at him, and quickly turned her head, returning it only when he was safely standing beside her. Though that in itself had its disturbing aspects. He was so close she could now actually smell his aftershave. It tantalised her nose, drawing all her senses into an appalling awareness. Her skin prickled beneath her clothing; her palms grew moist and clammy.

She turned her nose away, but it was a useless gesture. The scent was all around her, invading, infiltrating. Somehow it made her doubly conscious of her own drab appearance, and particularly resentful that no attractive fragrance was wafting from her skin to disturb him!

Not that it would, she thought mutinously. Men like Stephen Chase didn't spend their lives lusting uncontrollably after women like herself. They might find an inexperienced little widow suitable as a temporary bedmate, but on the whole the rich men of this world had their appetites catered for by glamorous exotic creatures with names like Madeline who undoubtedly always had ultra-feminine perfume lingering around their pulse-points.

And what did Rhea have at home to make her smell like a desirable woman? Nothing except baby powder and cheap deodorant! Her one bottle of perfume, given to her by Milan the Christmas before his death had long since run out.

Guilt consumed her at this sudden thinking of her dead husband. She had never worried about perfume when Milan had been alive, had never had her mind filled with romantic fantasies then. Even now, all she could think of was Stephen bending down and pressing his lips to hers . . .

She shuddered and shut her eyes, miserable in her awareness of the hot shaft of yearning pulsating along her veins. The depth of her arousal sickened her, and she wondered whether Stephen Chase had sold his soul to the devil to give him such wicked powers over women.

'I gather the purpose of this organisation is chiefly to raise funds for the school,' he began, then waited.

Everyone assented by nods or murmurs of agreement.

'In that case, I think I would like to hear the treasurer's report. And then I would appreciate it if our Madame Secretary here would read the minutes of the corresponding meeting last year. If she has them . . .'

She could feel his eyes boring down at her, but had no intention of raising her own. 'They're here somewhere,' she muttered. 'It will take me a few moments to locate them.' She began flipping through the book.

His sigh showed impatience and Rhea felt a surge of returned anger. What did he think this was, a fancy board meeting with her cast as his super-secretary?

'We'll use the time to hear from our treasurer,' he went on efficiently. 'Betty, wasn't it?'

Rhea looked up in time to see him throw Betty a heart-stopping smile. The silly woman preened, batting her lashes at him like a coy schoolgirl.

Rhea squirmed inside when Betty virtually simpered her way through the report. Everyone else, however, seemed more embarrassed by the contents rather than the treasurer's gushing manner.

The upshot was that the Association's bank balance stood at the pathetic amount of eighty-seven dollars and ten cents. The previous year had not been a good one, what with a break-in at the school and a disastrous fire in the store-room that had destroyed all the sports equipment.

'I see,' Stephen said slowly as the final tally was announced.

Rhea felt irritated that everyone was looking somewhat uncomfortable, as such a reaction was not warranted. Yet it was only human, she conceded, to want to look prosperous in the eyes of such an obvious success story as the man standing before them. But, to give Stephen his due, he came to their rescue.

'I must say it's damned good to find an organisation that's not in the red these days,' he praised. 'I can see I shan't mind this job at all. Now if you'd asked me to take on the railways . . .' He wiped his brow in mock distress.

Everyone laughed, including Rhea.

He slanted her a look. 'Careful, Mrs Petrovic,' he muttered under his breath. 'You might give the impression that you actually approve of me!'

Oddly enough, his aside did not intimidate or unnerve her any more than she already was. Instead, she was suddenly charged by the crazy urge to spar with him. 'Oh, but I do, Mr Chase,' she countered sweetly, 'in the position of president.'

The corner of his mouth lifted in a mockery of a smile. 'But not as anything else, it seems.'

'I don't know what you mean,' she answered in a brilliant parody of Betty's put-on breathless voice.

A shiver of alarm ran up and down her spine when he

leant down close to whisper, 'I hope you've got a damned good reason for the ridiculous games you've been playing with me. If you think you——'

'I've found the minutes you wanted, Mr Chase,' she said loudly, cutting him off. 'Shall I begin?'

If looks could kill ...

'By all means.' He sat down with a thump.

When she hesitated he drummed up a wide smile, patted her hand and said with exaggerated condescension, 'Now don't be nervous, my dear. We're all friends here, aren't we?'

Rhea wanted to hit him. Her hand actually itched with the effort of keeping it down. Instead, she smiled sweetly, then began to read.

She was a good reader, with an expressive musical voice, but it was rather hard to perform well with such a storm of emotions warring inside her. Still, she did her best, for it was important to her not to let Stephen undermine what she knew she could do well. She certainly didn't want to look a fool, as Betty had done.

At the end, she made sure she dropped her voice, not falling into the trap of finishing with a rising inflexion as so many women did, then calmly closed the book.

'Excellent,' murmured Stephen, and when she looked up she could see he was not mocking her in any way. The flush of pleasure she felt at his approval unnerved her more than anything had that evening.

With slow deliberation he rose to his feet once more. 'Hmm . . . I think the first thing we have to do is get the community working more solidly together in our fund-raising efforts. We have sixteen people here tonight and yet the school has approximately one hundred and thirty pupils, I'm told. Clearly involvement on a parental level is not overly high.'

Betty cleared her voice.

'You wish to say something, Betty?' Stephen offered.

She shifted in her seat, smiling coyly. 'Well . . .'

'Please.' He waved her to her feet and reseated himself.

'I think, Mr Chase,' Betty ventured, a smug expression on her quite pretty face, 'that we do have a problem with most of the parents not knowing each other. I mean, we all live on acreages out here and it sometimes takes *years* even before you get to know your neighbour.' She hesitated, making certain Stephen knew she didn't want it to take that long to get to know him! 'And there are so many new folk moving in all the time now . . .' She stopped suggestively, and Rhea could have sworn she fluttered her eyelashes again. She wanted to crawl into a hole and die of embarrassment for the whole female race.

'So what do you suggest? Some more social gatherings to get to know each other?'

'That would be marvellous!' gushed Betty. 'We had a bush dance one year——'

'And when it rained,' Rhea inserted bluntly, 'only a few people turned up and we lost money.'

'Did you sell the tickets beforehand?' Stephen asked, disarming Rhea with his businesslike manner.

'No,' she conceded reluctantly. 'It was pay at the door.'

'Always a mistake. People are fickle creatures. They're more likely to turn up if they've already paid, regardless of the weather. But a bush dance sounds just the thing, Betty. How about you all throw some ideas at me and we'll discuss it?'

It was a lively talk, and a very productive one. Everyone seemed in agreement that a bush dance would be a good start, and each person was allotted a specific task, from booking the band to providing bales of straw as decoration for the local community hall.

Stephen himself took on the job of having proper tickets printed, which would be sent home with each pupil and distributed through all local retail outlets. There was to be a barbecue and a fantastic raffle, prize to be supplied—again by Stephen.

It seemed he meant to be a generous president, although Rhea reserved judgement on this aspect of his character. It was easy to throw money around when one had oodles.

The clock on the wall chimed nine-thirty.

'I think we'd better wrap this meeting up,' Stephen decided. 'Nothing worse than meetings that go on too long on a work night.'

'My wife's prepared supper in the staffroom for anyone who wants it,' the headmaster announced.

Rhea hung back as everyone began filing out for the short walk to the tiny staffroom next door. Her plan was to sneak out, grab Emily and head for home before anyone noticed. Meanwhile, she stayed where she was, seated at the desk, pretending to be organising her records.

The trouser legs were grey this time, but they belonged to the same man.

Her chin lifted as though it were connected to a puppet string. He was glaring down at her, his face like granite.

'Come along, Mrs Petrovic,' he said brusquely.

'You're dragging the chain again. And there I was before tonight thinking you were perfect!'

Her heart sank, all her earlier bravado dissolving into mush. 'Stephen, I . . . I . . .' She fell silent, her mind and tongue no longer connected.

'What? Nothing to say? No advice to offer? No criticism to make? No more *lies* to tell? Good God, I'll have to mark this day down on my calendar!'

Rhea flinched at his anger. 'I meant to tell you,' she managed haltingly. 'But . . . but the time was never right.'

The anger in his face faded, replaced by a confused exasperation. 'Now that I can't fathom at all. Why on *earth* couldn't you just have said right from the beginning that your husband was dead? The whole thing is beyond comprehension. If you only knew what I——' He broke off, clearly at the end of his tether with her. 'What stuns me is how you thought you'd get away with it. You must have known I would find out. So why, Rhea, why?'

There was no excuse she could possibly make, except the truth. And that was far too humiliating—and revealing. She turned away from his probing glare to put the minutes book into her bag.

His sharp intake of breath had her whirling to face him. She was taken aback to see his eyes blinking wide with realised horror.

'It was because of *me*, wasn't it?' he accused. 'You don't want to get involved with someone like *me*!'

There was little use denying it when a betraying heat was already claiming her cheeks.

'What in God's name do you think I am?' he gasped. 'Some sort of ogre?' He was clearly bewildered to the point of real distress.

'Hey, Steve! Rhea!' Don called from the doorway. 'Leave that chit-chat and come and have a cup of coffee. The wife wants to wash up and get home before midnight!'

'Coming,' Stephen returned with a quick smile.

He sighed as he turned back to face her. 'Common sense tells me to walk away from you, Rhea—you're a very mixed-up lady. But I've never been large on common sense where women are concerned. I want you, Rhea. And I mean to have you, make no mistake about that. You can lie and play games till the cows come home, but one day, madam, you are going to be in my bed, ready and willing.'

Rhea listened to these incredible words with an ever-increasing pulse-rate, all the time telling herself that this wasn't happening. No man said things like that to a woman. Not out loud. Not here, in a lighted classroom. It was shocking!

But oh, so exciting . . .

The heat that had earlier invaded her face leapt to boiling-point.

'And now,' Stephen went on, a coldly satisfied smile coming to his face as he surveyed her telling blush, 'you and I are going to have a cup of coffee. Together!'

CHAPTER SEVEN

RHEA'S thoughts were tumbling every which way as Stephen propelled her from the classroom. What he had just said to her seemed even more incredible with every passing second. If he did mean it, then it made a mockery of his outrage at discovering why she might have lied to him. He had virtually just corroborated her opinion of his attitude to women—which had the unexpected bonus of putting a halt to any feelings of love she might have imagined she was harbouring for the man. *Love* Stephen Chase? Impossible! She made up her mind then and there that, no matter what her body felt about him, no matter what he said or did, she was not going to have an affair with him!

Nevertheless, she was relieved to reach the safety of the crowded staffroom, believing he wouldn't dare to say or do anything embarrassing in front of the others.

Don descended on them immediately with a cup of coffee each, then proceeded to regale Stephen with words of praise and gratitude at his taking on the presidency.

Everyone else wanted to speak to Stephen personally as well, keeping Rhea's fears of being somehow cornered by him at bay. Even so, he managed to keep her at his side, exuding a proprietorial manner towards her that she found perversely flattering.

Betty looked pea-green with envy, while the others were merely curious to find out exactly what relationship their normally man-shy Rhea had with their new president.

It seemed that Stephen's being a single father was no secret, neither was the surprising news that he was a tourist resort developer of some fame. Rhea was not a magazine or newspaper reader, so she wasn't familiar with the rich and famous of Sydney. When several people made allusions to his many property deals and his company—Chase Investments—she was left feeling stunned and ignorant. She found herself looking at him with even more wariness, this added knowledge reaffirming her belief that all he would ever want from her was sex.

Rhea knew she should excuse herself from his company, perhaps even go home, but she didn't. She stayed with him, looking and listening, watching and waiting, intrigued by the magnetism of the man. She was flirting with danger and she knew it.

As supper drew to a close, several couples having already departed, Rhea was to wish she had been more aloof. Without warning, Stephen slipped an arm around her waist, drawing her to his side, an intimate hand remaining on her hip. Her whole body stiffened, her eyes flying to him in outrage.

But his attention was focused on the couple they were talking to.

'I know they had to put the new airport somewhere,' Don's wife was saying, 'and it's far enough away not to be too noisy, but still . . . I don't think I like progress.'

'It's useless to fight against what's inevitable,' Stephen advised. 'Isn't it, Rhea?' He gave her a little squeeze and a quick smile.

Perhaps his only intention was to bring her into the

conversation, but Rhea didn't think so. His words clearly held a double meaning. The thought that he could be so boldly presumptuous of her capitulation gave Rhea the courage to move away from his touch, even though it only looked as if she was replacing her empty teacup in the sink against the wall.

'I don't think people should ever be apathetic,' she said coolly over her shoulder. 'They should stand up for what they believe in, and not allow minorities or governments to push them around.' She turned and fixed Stephen with a steady eye. 'I've often thought *progress* was a word coined by the greedy money-makers of this world. It often has little to do with the common good.'

He held her eyes, cocking his head slightly to one side. He would have to be stupid, Rhea decided, not to be getting her underlying messages.

'There again, I'm old-fashioned, I guess,' she went on. 'I still believe in things like marriage, which probably makes me an anachronism these days. People seem to drift in and out of relationships with all the thought some folk give to their purchases at the supermarket.' Rhea looked Stephen square in the eye. 'Most choices there are based on what's packaged best or what's closest at hand, which is hardly the way to find quality.'

An uncomfortable silence had descended on the group with Rhea's speech. Stephen continued to stare at her in puzzlement till finally Don cleared his throat and announced that poor Mrs Fraser would be wondering what was happening tonight and it was high time they all went home.

Leaving was fractionally easier than arriving. Once Laura and Emily joined them Stephen had no more opportunity to make any hair-raising comments, though he did give Rhea another penetrating look when she hurriedly said goodnight. Then as she walked over and unlocked the van he said quite loudly, 'I'll give you a call tomorrow night.'

She spun round, her face bristling with indignation.

'About the arrangements for the bush dance,' he added, a sardonic smile coming to his lips.

'Can't we go and visit instead, Dad?' Laura implored. 'I'm dying to see Emily's dogs. She says one of them's going to have puppies soon.'

'Not on a week night, sweetie,' Stephen returned gently. 'You'll have to see the dogs some other time.'

'Oh . . .'

Rhea was moved by the little girl's disappointment, but how could she invite her around without including the father?

'Couldn't Laura come home from school with me on the bus tomorrow, Mum?' Emily suggested. 'Then we could drop her at home when you go up the road to buy the oats and hay. We've run out, remember?'

Rhea sighed. Yes, she remembered—now that she'd been reminded. Just lately she would have forgotten her head if it wasn't screwed on. And the reason for her absent-mindedness was standing right before her.

'Would that be all right, Stephen?' she asked tautly.

His returning look carried surprise. 'If it's all right with you .'

She nodded wearily, having accepted that once again she was in a corner.

'I won't be home till six at least,' he added, walking over closer. 'Would that be too late?'

'No.'

'Perhaps you and Emily would like to come for dinner? It would be easy enough to tell Mrs King——'

'No, thank you,' Rhea cut in chillingly before the girls could jump on the bandwagon. 'I really can't spare the time—I have some urgent work I have to finish tomorrow night. But thank you for inviting us. Some other time, perhaps.'

Stephen gave her a tight, dry little smile. 'You will, however, stay long enough for coffee this time, won't you?'

'Of course,' she returned stiffly. 'We have to talk about the dance.'

That smile was hovering again. 'Ah, yes, the dance. . . '

'Goodnight, Mr . . . Stephen,' she amended, though curtly.

'Goodnight . . . Rhea.'

Before she could object he strode over and opened the van door for her. She had no option in front of the children but to get in, and, while she kept her eyes glued to the steering-wheel, she was sure he was looking at her legs, and the way the jeans pulled tight around her thighs as she climbed in.

Her cheeks felt hot and she was grateful when he swung the door shut, plunging the cabin into darkness. She shouldn't have unwound the window and glanced up to thank him, but she did and, whatever he read on her face, it took all the tension out of his.

'My pleasure,' he drawled, leaning his hands on the

window and bending towards her. 'See you at six tomorrow,' he said, grey eyes narrowing till they were nothing more than slits of wicked intent.

Rhea stared up into them, captivated, enthralled this time by *his* physical desire, not her own. He was staring at her mouth, staring as though he wanted to drink it dry, wanted to take it, to possess and seduce it with a mastery learnt from many years of experience . . .

Her lips parted with a soft moan.

'Mum? Have you lost your key or something?'

Rhea's eyes fell to the floor at Emily's voice and she fumbled with the ignition. God give me strength, she prayed.

But her hands were quivering as she fired the engine, her heart pounding madly. And, despite her earlier resolves of virtuous resistance, she knew—in that place reserved for the bitterest of truths—that she was already on the slippery slide to hell.

CHAPTER EIGHT

'BLUE suits you,' were the first words Stephen said to Rhea the following evening. He had been coming out of the double garage as she arrived, looking startlingly handsome in a charcoal-grey suit. On seeing her, he deposited his briefcase in the boot of the car and strode forward, opening her door and simultaneously giving forth with the smooth compliment about the colour of her silk dress.

Rhea gave him a cool look in reply.

'I hope Laura was no trouble,' he went on, taking her arm as she alighted from the van, his eyes running appreciatively over her figure.

She pulled away from his touch as swiftly as good manners would allow. 'No trouble at all.'

'Laura's got to go down and feed Mimi, Mum,' Emily told her as the girls scrambled from the passenger side. 'Can I go with her?'

'Oh . . .' Rhea had planned on keeping the children close by. 'All right, but don't be too long. I have to be home by seven at the latest.'

Stephen looked at his watch. 'It's already ten past six. That doesn't give us very long to talk.'

She lifted sharp eyes. 'It won't take all that long to finalise plans for the dance.'

He held her with a long uncompromising look. 'It wasn't only the dance I wanted to talk to you about, Rhea, as you very well know.'

Her stomach somersaulted. Surely he wasn't going to

start saying the same sort of thing today as he had last night?

'Do you have to look so damned scared?' Stephen flung at her in reproach. 'Look, Rhea, I . . . Oh, what the hell, I'm wasting my time making an apology, aren't I?' He muttered something more under his breath, then, taking her arm again, shepherded her into the plush-carpeted hallway.

'Mr Chase?' called a female voice. 'Is that you?'

'Yes, Mrs King.'

A portly woman in her fifties bustled into the hall, wiping her hands on a brightly flowered apron. 'Your dinner's all ready in the oven and—— Oh, sorry,' she broke off, noticing Rhea. 'I didn't realise you were going to have a visitor. Dear me, there's only enough food for ——'

'It's all right, Mrs King,' Stephen soothed. 'Mrs Petrovic's not staying.' These last few words had an edge to them, making Rhea feel guilty.

'Mrs Petr . . . goodness me! Then you're Emily's mother. Laura talks of no one else but Emily and you, isn't that so, Mr Chase?'

'Indubitably,' he said drily.

'It was so kind of you to look after her the day she ran off, Mrs Pet . . . Mrs P . . .' the woman laughed. 'I don't seem to be able to get my tongue around your name! Anyway, you look too young to be a Mrs with a ten-year-old daughter.'

Rhea blushed. 'That's very kind of you to say so. Call me Rhea, please . . .'

'Then you must call me Maisie. I don't fancy Mrs King much.' She cast a sheepish look at her boss at this announcement.

Stephen sighed. 'For pity's sake, then why haven't

you said so, Mrs K . . . Maisie?'

Maisie shrugged. 'It didn't seem proper, I suppose, you being my employer and all.'

Stephen made a disgruntled sound.

'Now now, Mr Chase, don't go getting all uptight over a silly name! You must be very tired. He was up at five this morning, love,' Maisie directed at Rhea, 'to catch an early flight to Brisbane, then he rushed home to be here for Laura. You know what happens to these people who burn the candle at both ends . . .' She wagged a motherly finger at Stephen. 'Now why don't you two pop along to the living-room and I'll bring you both a nice cup of coffee, eh? Or shall I get you something stronger?'

Stephen sighed again and Rhea could see he did look tired. 'Coffee will do fine. If I had a Scotch I don't think I'd stop at one. As for Mrs Petrovic . . .' he shot her a cynical look '. . . I doubt she would even dream of sullying her body with anything as poisonous as alcohol, would you, Rhea?'

Rhea could feel the heat zooming back into her cheeks, but she met him, eye for eye, not noticing the housekeeper's surprised expression. 'I've been known to try a drop or two occasionally,' she said defiantly, thinking of the sherry she had downed one sleepless night, all to forget this infuriatingly aggravating man. 'But coffee will do for now.'

Stephen shrugged indifferently before turning to stride down the hall. Rhea had no option but to follow or be left standing there like an idiot.

She stopped in the doorway of the large living area, watching as her ungracious host flicked open his suit jacket and slumped down into one of the deep leather armchairs. He looked up at her with an exasperated expression and indicated the chair next to him. 'Come over and sit down.' He yanked his tie loose, then undid the top button of his shirt. 'You make me nervous, hovering in the doorway.'

Rhea was taken aback. 'Nervous?' she queried.

'Yes! Nervous!'

'I'm sure you never feel nervous, Stephen Chase,' she stated primly, walking stiffly across the room and sitting down, totally unrelaxed with a straight back and clenched knees.

He sighed irritably. 'OK, so I'm behaving abominably. But you always make me feel so bloody inadequate!'

Her eyes snapped up in astonishment.

'That surprises you?' Stephen grated out. 'Don't worry, it surprises me too. I don't usually let women get under my skin.'

The oddest feelings claimed her stomach, a mixture of satisfaction and anger. Satisfaction that she was at least affecting him in some way. Anger at his easy dismissal of any vital female role in his life.

Knowing how tell-tale her face could be, Rhea dropped her eyes, staring down at the floor in acute discomfort as the silence between them lengthened.

'Rhea?' he said at last.

'Yes?' She looked up when he didn't go on, only to find his gaze raking hers with disturbing penetration.

'Was I right?' he asked tautly. 'About why you lied to me?'

Rhea stared at him, searching her mind frantically for some way out. She hadn't seriously expected him to bring the subject up again today. But then she hadn't expected Emily to run off with Laura. She had planned to keep her daughter close—as protection.

She turned her face away, then stared back down at the floor, twisting her hands together in a nervous knot.

Stephen leant forward in his chair, bringing his face disturbingly close. She flinched back.

'For God's sake, woman, what are you frightened of?' he demanded, suddenly enclosing her hands in his. When she tried to snatch them away he held them fast. 'Do you think I'd hurt you?' he whispered thickly.

Rhea looked up at him with anguished eyes, knowing that she couldn't just sit there with his flesh around hers for much longer or her body would burst into flames. 'Please, Stephen, let me go,' she gasped. 'I . . . I'm not frightened of you. Please . . . I just don't like being touched . . . I came here today to discuss the dance, that's all.' She pulled back from his grasp, jerking back in the chair when he suddenly released her.

'Do you expect me to ignore how I feel about you?' he charged. 'Or how *you* feel about *me*?'

For an electric moment his words hung in mid-air. Rhea could feel her heart pounding in her chest, her whole being straining towards him. But she held firm and strong, believing that if she could get past this one trial she would be safe. 'And what is that,' she countered, 'except a passing attraction? I'm sorry, Stephen, but I'm not interested in casual sex, or one-night stands.'

'Neither am I,' he snapped impatiently.

'Oh? What are you offering, then—an affair?' Her voice was beginning to shake with emotion. 'Sorry, but that's not on either, Stephen. I *don't* want to become involved with you. And my reasons are my own.'

'What reasons?' Is it something to do with your husband, is that it? Do you think you're being disloyal to his memory? My God, Rhea, the man's been dead for six years!'

She flushed. So he *had* been making enquiries about her. 'That's not it,' she said truthfully.

'Then what, for pity's sake? Don't go pretending you're not attracted to me!'

His arrogance fired a resentful anger. 'Oh? Would that be so unlikely? Or do *all* women fall at your feet when you choose to turn your eye their way?'

An answering fury swept across Stephen's handsome face. 'Don't be ridiculous! I've never thought of myself as God's gift to women! Not only that, I work too damned hard to be worrying about sex every minute of the day. It isn't the be-all and end-all of my life.'

'That's not the impression you gave me last night when you virtually threatened to get me into your bed, by fair means or foul. I was shocked by that, Stephen. Truly shocked.'

His features took on a ravaged regret. 'I know ... Dear God, don't you think I know? I was angry and frustrated. I made a mistake ...'

'A mistake, Stephen? Or merely an error in tactics? Your aim is still the same. You want me in your bed.'

He gave her the oddest look. It was half grim, half exasperated. 'I can't deny that.'

'At least you're honest about it, I suppose. But let me be equally honest. I do find you attractive. You're an exceptionally attractive man, as you well know, but I have no intention of going to bed with you. Do I make myself clear?'

'Very clear,' he sighed, though he continued to glare at her for several seconds. No doubt he found her behaviour both annoying and incomprehensible. Despite what he'd said Rhea knew that women probably rarely rejected him.

Finally he leant back in his chair. 'There's not much point pursuing this subject, then, is there? About the catering . . .' And with a manner briskly efficient and businesslike he began tying up all the loose ends pertaining to the dance.

It was perverse of Rhea to be hurt by his sudden coldness towards her. She had asked for it, had rejected all his persistent and flattering attempts to seduce her. But hurt she was. Perhaps in the corner of her female mind she had wanted him to pursue her with a passion that brooked no opposition, literally sweep her off her feet and carry her up to bed, thereby taking all responsibility for her actions away from her.

'What are you going to have as the raffle prize?' she asked in a flat little voice. 'I'd like to be able to say what it is in the school bulletin.'

'How about a saddle?' Stephen suggested. 'Or an open order at the nearest saddlery for five hundred dollars. Everyone around here seems horse-mad.'

'Five hundred dollars!' She frowned. 'That's an awful lot, isn't it?'

He shrugged. 'I can afford it. Ah, here's the coffee.'

'Sorry I took so long,' chirped Maisie as she waddled into the room with a tray. 'I thought I'd put the kettle on, but it was turned off at the power-point.' She placed the tray on the coffee-table and began taking off her apron, totally oblivious of the tension in the room. 'I have to fly, Mr Chase. Bingo starts down at the club at seven-thirty and I have to change.'

Stephen reached into the breast pocket of his suit and drew out his wallet. He extracted a selection of notes. 'A little extra, Mrs K . . . Maisie . . . for all your overtime.'

'Oh, Mr Chase, you needn't!' she protested.

'You deserve it. Now off you go and have a good time. Breakfast at six tomorrow, OK?'

'You really are a kind man, Mr Chase.' Maisie beamed her approval at him, then smiled at Rhea. 'Nice to have met you, love.'

As Maisie hurried from the room Stephen looked at Rhea. 'Don't worry,' he drawled coldly once they were alone, 'you don't have to think well of me for any of my supposedly generous gestures. I donate money to a hundred different charities, mostly for tax reasons, and I always bribe my house staff. Then I don't have to feel guilty about asking a little extra of them.'

'It's none of my business what you do, Stephen,' she said unhappily, 'though I'm sure everyone at the P & C will be very grateful for your donation to the raffle.'

'But not you.'

The uncomfortable moment was saved by Emily and Laura running up to the back porch and opening the sliding doors. 'It's raining again,' Laura announced as they both skipped inside.

Stephen scowled. 'Damn it! I hate flying in bad weather.'

'Where are you going to tomorrow, Dad?' Laura asked, sitting on the arm of his chair and winding her small arm around his neck.

He flipped her curls. 'Back to Brisbane, poppet.'

'But you were up there today!'

'That's life,' he sighed. 'Problems with a bank manager—not to mention the local council. They seem determined to block a road I need.'

'I wish I could come too,' she complained.

'You have to go to school. Now, how about taking Emily into the kitchen for a lemonade while her mother and I have this coffee? It's getting cold.'

Both girls gave them a curious look before racing from the room, giggling as they went.

'I hate the sound of girls giggling,' Stephen muttered after them before picking up the coffee-pot to pour. 'Milk and no sugar, isn't it?' he said, flicking Rhea a swift glance.

She nodded, feeling depressed that he seemed to be avoiding looking at her now. 'You have a good memory,' she remarked.

One corner of his mouth lifted in a wry smile. 'I'm good at most things,' he said, and handed her the cup.

Rhea took the cup with slightly shaking fingers, trying desperately to ignore the way her thoughts had taken flight at his comment. She was relieved when the phone rang, requiring Stephen to stand up and move away.

He strode quickly across the room to swoop up the receiver from the table in a corner. 'Yes?' he asked in a brisk tone. A brief silence ensued, then she heard him sigh, deeply. 'Madeline, I thought we had this out before . . .' His back was to Rhea, but in the silent room even his low tones carried well. 'I see . . . all right . . . I suppose I can manage that . . .'

Rhea's mouth went dry as she listened unhappily to the one-sided conversation. Undoubtedly Madeline was trying to patch up their relationship. Which wasn't surprising; Rhea couldn't imagine a woman getting over Stephen in a hurry. Somehow she could hear the unhappy woman's desperation, begging her ex-lover to see her again, asking for one more chance, settling for some lukewarm acceptance of her invitation. It was totally humiliating, and only served to remind Rhea what lay in store for her if she fell victim to this man's charms. Not that she hadn't already . . .

'. . . Very well, I'll meet you in front of the theatre . . . around seven . . . Don't worry if I'm a bit late . . . That's perfectly all right . . . I understand . . . What was that . . . ? You could be right . . .'

Unexpectedly he laughed. It had a soft sensual sound to it that curled through Rhea's stomach, stabbing her with a fierce jealousy. A wild urgent voice clamoured in her brain to go to him, to tell him he didn't need Madeline, that she, Rhea, would give him what he wanted, anywhere, any time!

Rhea drained the coffee-cup and got unsteadily to her feet. It was definitely time for her to go.

'You always were persuasive, Maddie dear,' he was saying teasingly. He gave another low laugh. 'But don't push your luck! See you Friday. Bye.'

He hung up and turned, a weary resignation sweeping across his face when he saw Rhea ready to leave. 'I'll see you out,' he said in clipped tones.

Rhea held herself proud and tall. 'There's no need.'

'Nevertheless . . .' He turned sharply on his heel and preceded her to the door, calling to the girls on the way.

Rhea made it all the way home and into the bathroom before the tears came.

CHAPTER NINE

THE DAY of the bush dance arrived without producing in Rhea the nerves that had preceded her other meetings with Stephen. Her feelings for him had reached a crisis point on the Friday night two weeks previously, the night of his date with Madeline.

Rhea had been watching the late-night news on television when there was a brief spot covering the première of a new musical that night at the Capitol Theatre. As the camera swung over the crowd tumbling out after the performance Rhea glimpsed both Stephen and the blonde from the airport, confirming in Rhea's mind exactly which blonde Madeline was. Neither appeared to mind the way the crowd were crushing them up against each other.

Upset, Rhea had paced her bedroom for hours, torturing herself with visions of their making love together later. At the crack of dawn she had literally hauled Emily out of bed, packed up the small van, fed and watered the animals, then driven down to Kiama.

Her mother had been astonished though delighted to see them, although she soon noticed her daughter's agitation. Rhea had never been a good confider, however, and after a few tentative attempts at probing at the problem her mother didn't press. She and Bill took Emily down to the beach and left Rhea to cry out her misery in private.

Rhea was surprised how nice Bill was to her during her weekend stay, fussing over her and buying her a bottle of white wine because he knew she disliked the beer he normally stocked. She had been touched, going so far as to join him in a mild drinking session that Saturday night. It was the first time in her life that she had felt comfortable in his company, and she really appreciated his genuine attempts at cheering her up.

She found herself looking at her stepfather with different eyes. He seemed genuinely moved by her warmer manner towards him, all of which made her feel more than a fraction guilty. What had she ever done to deserve his affection? Not much.

It was good, too, to be able to watch him touch her mother without cringing inside. Rhea's new understanding gave her an insight into their relationship that the teenage Rhea had not had a hope of appreciating. They clearly loved each other, with a deep and passionate love, a love which could not always confine itself to the bedroom.

Rhea could see now that her upbringing prior to her father's death had set her on a path to physical shyness which she was only now getting over. Her father had never been one to hug and kiss, not even in the privacy of home. He had been a silent, reserved man, a man not given to sentiment or emotional love, or the physical demonstrations of them. Milan had been much the same, Rhea realised with another burst of enlightenment. He had confined his attentions to her till the lights were out at night, not liking to even hold hands in public.

By the time she began the drive home on the Sunday, Rhea had achieved a satisfying mental peace regarding Bill and her mother. Not so regarding Stephen. She could see no solution to her problem, particularly now Madeline was back on the scene, not forgetting the young woman in the coffee lounge. Who was to say Stephen wasn't still sleeping with her as well?

Rhea might have succumbed to the temptation of an affair with Stephen if she'd been the only woman in his life, but she could not commit herself to such intimacy with a man who the very next night could be doing the same thing with another woman. That would tear her apart.

By the time she reached Banagloo Creek she had resolved to cut him out of her mind and heart, totally, irrevocably. She wasn't in love with him yet, of that she was almost sure. The balance of her feelings was still on the physical side. It was a case of mind over matter, she believed.

Oddly enough, she almost succeeded, but as she did so a depression descended, heavy and sluggish, so that everything she did was an enormous effort. She felt tired all the time. Not agitated as she had been before, just bone-weary.

By sheer force of will she finished her autumn range of knitwear, the last garment being pressed and delivered the day before the bush dance. The troublesome red top had never made the grade, however. It had finally been discarded, thrown into the bottom of a drawer with a few other rejects, most of which she eventually resurrected for wearing herself.

One of them, a crocheted top of natural mohair and raw silk—suffering from a slight stain—was Rhea's selection for the bush dance. A couple of weeks back she might have gone out and splurged on a new outfit, pretending it was not to impress Stephen but underneath knowing it was.

Now, she didn't seem to care. A pair of her old jeans would do, along with her high-heeled ankle-boots, bought when they were in fashion years before.

Rhea pulled on the stone-washed jeans she had chosen and struggled to do up the zipper. Damn, she thought irritably, why did cheap clothes always have to shrink when you washed them? She turned side-on and looked at herself in the mirror, a grimace curling her lips at the way the stretch denim hugged her figure. Thank goodness the top came down over her hips, hiding most of the displayed curves.

Rhea sighed and turned her attention to her hair. It was being its usual stubborn self, refusing to be easily tamed. She brushed it vigorously before corralling the mass high on her head with a tight elastic band. She was just about to secure it with pins when Emily came into the room.

'Oh, Mum, don't!' she exclaimed. 'It looks great! The pins will only come out when you dance anyway and then it'll look messier.'

'I have no intention of dancing,' Rhea pronounced, suddenly worried that Stephen might ask her if he saw her on the floor. She might have discarded him from her day-to-day thoughts, but that didn't mean she would survive being imprisoned in his arms.

'But what if someone asks you to?' asked Emily with a little giggle. 'You can't be rude and say no. That's what you told me.' Her face was split with a mischievous grin.

Rhea gave her daughter a sharp look. What was she up to? Had she and Laura inveigled Stephen into asking her to dance? She prayed not. 'I . . . I'll be too busy with the supper to dance,' she said, almost defensively.

Emily said nothing, but as she left the room she was still smiling.

'My, my, don't you look sexy!' was the first thing Betty Waymouth said to her that evening.

Rhea glanced up in astonishment from where she was preparing salad in the small servery attached to the community hall. 'Sexy?' She glanced down incredulously at her old jeans and crocheted top.

'You haven't got a bra on, have you?' Betty said slyly.

Rhea blinked. 'Of course I have.' She stared down at her front, noting for the first time that her flesh-coloured underwear did blend in with the natural colours of the raw silk and mohair top.

'Have you seen Stephen yet?' Betty went on. 'He's out helping set up the barbecue. God, he looks gorgeous! I thought he might be one of those suit men—you know, the kind that need to be dressed formally to look good —but what that man can do for a pair of tight jeans is wicked!'

'I'm sure Mr Chase would be thrilled with your observation,' muttered Rhea. Talking about the man seemed to be reviving all those old breathless feelings. It was very annoying.

Betty laughed mockingly. 'And I'm sure you don't call him Mr Chase when you're having one of your cosy little meetings, do you? Come on, do tell!' She came up to Rhea and leant close. 'What's he like in bed? Fantastic, I'll bet!'

Rhea recovered from her initial shock at such impertinence to give Betty a withering look. 'I really wouldn't know.'

The other woman merely shrugged. 'Not telling, eh?'

'There's *nothing* to tell! Look, Betty, why don't you make yourself useful and start helping me cut up this salad?'

'Sorry, I've already promised Stephen I'll help on the barbecue,' Betty said airily as she swept from the hall.

Rhea shook her head and set to work, determinedly ignoring the apprehensive gnawing in her stomach.

She managed to avoid seeing Stephen during the preparations for the dance. Not consciously. It just happened. Though it did cross her mind once that perhaps he was deliberately avoiding her. The thought hurt much more than it should have, she realised uneasily, if she were truly over him.

By eight o'clock the dance was in full swing, with the barbecue sizzling, the band booming, feet tapping, people dancing and drinking, eating and laughing. The supper was all perfectly prepared and laid out, leaving Rhea no further excuse to hide in the servery. But she felt too strung up to go and join in the dancing, deciding instead to step outside the hall for a breath of fresh air.

She squeezed past the group of people standing smoking around the entrance and walked slowly down the wide front steps, stopping on the last one to look back up at the coloured lights hanging along the guttering. They lent a real party atmosphere, and the music pounding out from the windows had a marvellously invigorating sound.

'I think we could call it an unqualified success, don't you?'

Stephen's voice emerging from nowhere spun Rhea

around. She stared at the emptiness of the surroundings in bewilderment till he suddenly stepped out from the shadow of a nearby tree.

'You nearly scared me to death!' she reproached, a defensive hand fluttering to her throat.

He didn't make any attempt to cross the few paces between them. 'I appear to have that effect on you all the time,' he drawled.

She gave a nervous laugh. 'Don't be silly!'

He took one step towards her, bringing him into better light. Rhea swallowed. Betty had not been exaggerating. What he did to jeans was wicked!

'You were certainly right about selling the tickets beforehand,' she chattered away. 'We've got a big roll-up. Though it's just as well we organised a separate dance for the kids up in the classrooms. This hall couldn't have coped with the children as well.'

She was well aware that she was babbling on, but Stephen was standing far too close, watching her far too intently.

'I still make you nervous, don't I?' he said slowly.

She lifted panicky eyes. 'Please don't start anything, Stephen. I thought we'd come to an understanding.'

He gave a dry laugh. 'You might have come to an understanding, Rhea, but I certainly haven't.'

Her hand reached up to rub the base of her throat. It was a nervous habit of hers, but it drew his gaze. When her hand moved lower, to rest half frozen in the valley between her breasts, his eyes followed. Hot lights blazed deep in their grey depths, telling her he still wanted her. She tried to control the mad response of her heart by reminding herself that he didn't keep his virility exclusively for her. But somehow that thought didn't work this time. Her breasts were swelling under his searing glare, the rock-hard tips pressing painfully against her bra.

'Come inside and dance with me,' he invited huskily.

Rhea stood frozen, watching with wide eyes as he reached out his hand towards her.

'Don't say no,' he almost pleaded.

Rhea realised dazedly that it was this soft tactic he often employed that was so appealing. There was no grabbing, pushing, forcing. He got what he wanted with a seductive persuasiveness that was more tempting than the most macho approach.

Without her making a conscious decision, her hand seemed to find his. She was unnerved by the smile on his face when it did so. Perhaps she might have understood triumph. But this was relief, a gut-wrenching relief combined with such joy that all Rhea's preconceptions about this man were shaken. Could it be possible that he really cared about her? came the astonishing thought.

Her lips moved back in a tentative smile. 'I . . . I'm not familiar with square dancing,' she murmured. 'I won't know what to do.'

'That's all right,' Stephen reassured her in a low, gentle voice. 'Just follow me.'

He led her up the steps, carefully making a path for her through the crowd, protecting her from any jostling. A rigorous reel was in progress, the movements looking complicated. They joined the group nearest, Rhea's attention swinging away from Stephen as she concentrated on picking up the steps.

It was easy really, after the first time. At the beginning of the round partners faced each other in two parallel lines. With hands behind their own backs they surged forward, retreating before they actually touched. Then the couple at the head of the lines held hands and skipped sideways down the aisle till they reached the end, while the other clapped, at which point the pairs surged forward again, this time linking arms and going into a vigorous spin. Then the whole procedure was repeated, with a different couple this time at the head of the lines.

No dance could have been more simple, or less erotic. So Rhea mistakenly thought in the beginning.

It was the eye contact, of course. From his vantage-point opposite Stephen stared at her the whole time, his half-lidded gaze incredibly sensuous. When he surged towards her, she felt as if she were literally burning under the heat of his scrutiny. She found herself holding her breath, waiting for the brief moments when he dropped his eyes to her breasts, which were too well rounded to be sedately still while dancing.

Even when he spun her round his head twisted to one side to keep her eyes locked to his, making her continually conscious of what he wanted of her.

It was agony. And ecstasy.

Heaven. And hell.

She was sure people were watching them, sure they could see the interplay between them. But with each passing round, each nerve-shattering contact, she gradually ceased to care.

In the end the crowd and the other dancers receded totally from her conscious mind. It was all Stephen,

Stephen, Stephen. Rhea knew she was looking back at him with an equally hungry gaze, but she didn't care, she didn't care. She was too aroused, too besotted with those tempting grey eyes, that tantalisingly virile male body, to appreciate the disastrous depth of her susceptibility.

Even before the music died, he was sweeping her outside the hall, drawing her into the shadows of the trees, pressing the heated length of her against a tree-trunk, holding her shoulders captive, bending his lips to hers.

Why she turned her face away at the last moment, she didn't know. It wasn't because she was resisting him—she was past that. It was just one of those instinctive gestures.

His lips landed on her neck. He groaned, then sucked at her flesh with a primitive, almost ravenous ferocity. A sob of naked desire caught in Rhea's throat.

His hands were already moving over her body, tracing the lush curves, making her shiver uncontrollably. 'I thought you didn't like to be touched,' he growled deep in his throat. And with slow deliberation he leant against her, moulding his aroused body to hers, rubbing himself against her. Her breathing grew more ragged. Her skin felt seared.

'You're a witch, do you know that?' he breathed huskily. 'A teasing, tormenting witch.'

His fingers intertwined with hers and he slowly wound her hands back, back, till they were pressed against the bark behind her, with no leverage to escape his physical domination of her.

Not that she wanted to. Her whole body was like a

furnace, burning for him.

'Kiss me, Rhea. Kiss me . . .'

Why did he ask? He took her mouth without waiting, expecting no further opposition. So he was taken aback to find her lips pressed sedately shut.

'Don't play any more games with me, for God's sake.' His voice was thick with passion. 'Open your mouth!'

Rhea blinked up at him, for she had never ever kissed with her mouth open before. She had asked Milan about it once, having read about it several times in books. But he had told her that was the way sluts kissed, and men didn't want their wives kissing like that.

Stephen released one of her hands, bringing his own up to run a finger over her mouth, at first encircling the shape, then rubbing along the line between her lips. Quite involuntarily her tongue tip moved to meet it.

'Yes,' he groaned. 'Like that . . . That's what I want . . .'

This time when his head bent Rhea was more than ready to give him exactly what he wanted. And more . . .

Her lips parted willingly, hungrily, the invasion of his tongue kindling a passion in her which till now she had only suspected lay inside her. Somehow her hands found their way around his neck, her fingers twisting into the thick black curls as she pulled him down to her, wanting him closer and closer, his tongue deeper and deeper.

A more experienced woman would have realised how far she was inviting him to go. His legs pushed between her thighs, his hands sliding down to cup her buttocks. In the deep state of her arousal she welcomed the feel of his hardness against her and without thinking she began to move wantonly against him. She was in another world, a world of heated flesh, and pulsating places.

The sound of nearby laughter catapulted her back to reality. 'Some people just can't wait, eh?' came the hideously truthful comment.

Rhea jerked upright, her action bringing a gasp of pain from Stephen.

'What the . . .?' Then he too heard the laughter. He swore softly under his breath before dragging in and expelling a single shuddering breath. 'They can't see us properly, you know,' he muttered, and drew her deeper into the shadows.

Rhea made a sound which must have shown how distressed she was, for he gathered her quickly into the deep haven of his arms, rocking her gently. 'Hush, darling, hush!' he whispered.

She was not crying, but she was trembling, so much so that her teeth were rattling.

'There, there,' he soothed with his incredible gentleness. 'Don't let those oafs bother you. So we got a little carried away . . .'

Rhea groaned.

'Hey!' He gave her a little shake. 'It's nothing to be ashamed of, you know.'

'Isn't it?' There was a wealth of misery in the words. For with the cooling of passion had come shame. She had vowed not to become involved with this man, but a clever smile, a sexy dance, and she'd been his for the taking. She was disgusted with herself!

Stephen pulled back and held her at arm's length,

gazing at her in the dim light with darkly troubled eyes. 'No, definitely not! Embarrassing perhaps to be interrupted publicly, but not shameful.'

'Maybe not for you,' she threw at him, face flushed, eyes tormented. 'You're probably used to doing things anywhere with anyone, but I . . . I'm . . . Oh, God!' She wrenched away from him, cradling her heated cheeks with shaking hands.

'Rhea . . .'

He went to take her in his arms again, but she fought him off in a panic. To have him touch her again would be inviting disaster. She closed her eyes and shuddered.

'You're acting like a little goose,' Stephen reproved, impatience in his voice. 'I agree that this is hardly the most appropriate place to attempt to assuage our mutual passion, but we didn't go through with it, so it's not the end of the world!'

Rhea's eyes flew open to stare at him, her mind awash with the implications of his coldly insensitive speech. And she had thought he might care for her! 'My God, but you are a bastard!' she rasped.

His hands shot out to close around her arms and he yanked her against his chest, grey eyes lancing her with the icy steel of anger. 'If I were the bastard you've always thought me, I would have had you long ago!'

'Why, you . . . you——'

'Don't bother with the insults,' he interrupted savagely. 'You know and I know that this . . . *attraction* . . . has been between us from the start, even when you were playing your little games. Though why you bothered, I don't know. Your having a husband wouldn't have kept a bastard at bay, would it?'

She groaned and tried to escape, but he held her fast, pushing her back up against the tree. 'I want you, Rhea,' he muttered thickly. He cradled her face in his hands, taking her mouth in a hard, hungry kiss. 'Hate me all you like, but you're going to let me make love to you one day. It's as inevitable as the day dawning!'

She opened her mouth to deny it, to argue, but he took her lips again, this time using every masterful technique of erotic persuasion his experience possessed.

It was hardly fair, with Rhea already in an advanced state of arousal. She tried to fight him, tried to resist, but it was useless and he sensed it. 'Rhea, Rhea, don't fight me . . . Just kiss me! Kiss me . . .'

And she did—madly, resignedly, desperately.

'Oh, darling, darling,' Stephen murmured against her swollen mouth. 'You want me too, don't you?'

A tiny tortured sound fluttered from her lips. Why did he need words from her when every vestige of her body was showing him her complete vulnerability? It was there in the way she was clinging to him, the way her body was afire for his touch.

A shiver raced up her spine.

'Don't be afraid of me, Rhea,' he whispered huskily. 'I won't hurt you, I promise . . . We'll take everything very slowly. All I want for now is to make love to you. All you have to do is let me . . .'

Rhea closed her eyes against his chest. She could hear his heart beating, as crazily and as loudly as her own. Perhaps she could have fought her own desire, but not his as well. It was like the ultimate drug, knowing that he wanted her with such intensity.

'Come out with me tomorrow night,' he urged.

'I can't!' she gasped, unable to cope with such immediacy.

'Why not?'

Why not? Why not? Her mind blurred till it grasped the first excuse she could think of. 'Emily . . .'

'. . . can sleep over with Laura,' he finished persuasively. 'Maisie will look after them.'

He tipped up her chin and looked her straight in the eye. 'I can't go on like this, Rhea,' he said fiercely. 'I want you so badly I ache all over. Say you'll be with me.'

'I . . . I . . .'

'Say it!'

'All right,' she gasped.

A light gleamed in his eyes and he drew her to him, his hands stroking her back. 'You won't regret it, darling,' he whispered, his lips in her hair. 'Never. Ever. It's going to be wonderful between us. Wonderful.'

Wonderful . . .

Full of wonder . . .

Rhea laid her dazed head against Stephen's chest, her brain indeed full of wonder. Was this all real? Was it happening to her? Had she really just said yes?

One part of her mind implored her to think again, to find a way to back out. The other had more insidious thoughts.

You want this man, Rhea. Want him in a way you have never known before. Why shouldn't you have him? Why shouldn't you experience, at least once, the pleasure, the satisfaction, he can give you? What harm could come of it?

It was a reasonable and very tempting line of

thinking, and one which she yearned to embrace. But somewhere at the back of her mind she knew that there was harm in it. For her.

'What is it?' Stephen murmured. 'You keep shivering. Are you cold?'

She shook her head with a deep shudder, hating herself for her weakness, but when he pulled back and stroked her cheek with a gentle hand any idea of potential danger went from her mind. It felt right when he touched her—more than right. It felt incredible.

He bent to kiss her again, softly this time, but even more seductively. 'I don't know how I'll be able to wait,' came his husky whisper when they finally drew apart. 'Tell me again you want me. Give me something to remember, to make the next twenty-four hours bearable.'

'I want you, Stephen,' she said shakily, nestling her face under his chin.

'I want you,' she repeated as her lips grazed his neck. 'Oh, how I want you!'

CHAPTER TEN

RHEA was awakened the next morning by her telephone ringing. She dragged herself out of bed, making it all the way down the hall before she remembered what had transpired at the dance.

She stopped dead in her tracks, at once appalled and incredulous as the vivid memories of her behaviour hit her. How could she have been so . . . so . . .? She must have been mad!

Visions of people staring at them when Stephen took her back into the hall made her cringe. She had been sure they all knew what they'd been doing. Sure!

Yet Stephen had carried himself off with such panache, smiling at everyone, drawing the raffle with a laugh, even flirting with a speechless Betty when she came up to accept the prize. *He* didn't feel embarrassed in the slightest. Oh, no, why should he? He was on familiar territory, seducing females probably being second nature to him.

What had he said to her in the shadows? All he wanted to do was make love to her . . . No mention of anything else, such as, 'You're special, Rhea, I like you, I could fall in love with you.' Heck, no! Just, 'All I want for now is to make love to you.' No promises, no commitment. Nothing more than a brief encounter!

And what had *she* done?

Wrapped herself around him like a clinging vine, confessing how much she wanted him, without pride or shame or the slightest reservation.

The sound of the phone's insistent ringing brought her self-reproach to a swift end. With a groan Rhea raced into the kitchen. It would be her mother ringing to check up on her. If only she knew!

Her hand hovered about the receiver as she pulled herself together, resolving with a quiet desperation not to let her panic show through in her voice. She was a grown woman now and had to stand on her own two feet, not let someone else bear the burden of her follies.

'Hi,' she breezed into the receiver.

'You sound happy this morning,' Stephen answered.

'Oh . . .' Her chest tightened, her thoughts instantly jumbled.

'I gather it wasn't me you were expecting,' he said, dry amusement in his voice.

'No, I . . . er . . . I . . .' Irritation at her bumbling firmed her voice. 'I thought you were my mother,' she stated with gritted jaw.

He laughed. 'Sorry. Lover here, not mother.'

Rhea almost curled up with embarrassment at the ease of his flirtatious banter. But she was determined to extricate herself from this unthinkable situation. It staggered her that she had put herself into it in the first place.

'Stephen, I'm glad you rang,' she began, nerves making her sound aggressive.

'No!'

She swallowed. 'No what?'

'No backing out. No cold feet. No! I want you, Rhea, more than I've ever wanted any woman. Now either you lied to me again last night or you want me just as much. Which is it?' he snarled.

Oh, God! Her head was pounding, whirling.

Stop fooling yourself! an inner voice dictated. Sooner or later you'll see him again, and this mad desire will take possession once more. Wanting him won't go away. It's like a sickness, an obsession. Say yes, Rhea, the crazy voice urged. Go to bed with him! Maybe it will burn itself out and you'll be able to get your life on an even keel once more.

'I won't let you, you know,' Stephen went on in a low, dangerous voice.

'Won't let me?' she gasped.

'Do this to yourself as well as me. You're coming out with me tonight if I have to come over there and drag you out by the hair!'

Rhea took a startled breath, the implacable force of Stephen's intent sweeping away all her wafflings, replacing them with an insidious excitement. She felt like a butterfly caught in a net after its last struggles for freedom had died. She was waiting, breathless with anticipation, for her fate.

'Rhea?'

'Yes?'

'I trust I won't have to do that.'

'No . . .'

There was a brief silence between them, the passing seconds charged with a crackling tension.

'Where . . . where are you taking me?' she asked at last.

'I have a place in town.'

So . . . There was to be no pretence of anything else. No romantic dinner first. Just straight down to business. The thought should have chilled Rhea. Instead, it aroused her — horribly so.

'I thought we'd have a couple of drinks there first,' Stephen went on briskly, 'then catch a taxi to a restaurant for dinner. Is that OK with you?'

A niggling thought insinuated that she had jumped to the wrong conclusion about him. Again. 'Yes . . . yes, that's all right.'

'You don't sound so sure.'

She could hardly tell him she didn't know what she thought or wanted any more. Except him.

She heard him sigh. 'I'll pick you up at six,' he pronounced, and hung up.

'Gosh, you look fantastic, Mum!' Emily exclaimed.

Rhea smiled tightly at her daughter, her nerves at breaking-point as the clock struck six. 'I'm glad you think so, love.'

'Laura's father is going to flip!'

Rhea had to admit she did look good, the troublesome red top suiting her, the slightly irregular neckline not even noticeable on her full-breasted figure. Though thank heaven Betty wasn't around to comment on the amount of cleavage on display, this time definitely with no bra!

'The black trousers turned out great, didn't they?' Emily complimented. 'Just as well you didn't have to play at a wedding today!'

Rhea agreed, having spent all afternoon making the trousers from a piece of black silk she owned. She had given the simple pull-on style a more elegant line by tapering the legs at the ankles.

'I'm glad you didn't put your hair up,' Emily went on gaily. 'You look ten years younger with it out like that.'

'Oh, thank you very much,' laughed Rhea, clutching

at any distraction. 'How old do I normally look?'

Emily grinned. 'About twenty-five.'

'And now I look fifteen?'

Emily giggled. 'Heavens, no! Oh, listen, I think I can hear Mr Chase's car coming. Gosh, I just can't wait! This is so exciting, my sleeping over and your going out with Laura's father. Maybe you and he will——'

'Go and get your bag, Emily,' Rhea cut in firmly. 'We don't want to keep Mr Chase waiting, do we?'

'Gosh, no!'

She raced off and Rhea closed her eyes. Her stomach was churning dreadfully, her heart galloping.

One of the dogs started barking as a car definitely turned into her drive.

'Oh, by the way, Mum,' said Emily on her return, 'I couldn't find Bobby and Dolly earlier when I went to feed them, so I put their food into their kennel, is that OK?'

'What? Oh, yes, that's fine.'

'The chooks are away, so it doesn't matter if the dogs aren't locked up,' Emily went on.

Rhea frowned at her daughter, not really hearing anything. She was listening for Stephen's footsteps, yet when his knock came she almost jumped out of her skin.

Gathering herself, she walked across and opened the door.

There was only one way to describe how he looked to her. Breathtaking! Dressed in tailored black trousers, a smoke-grey silk shirt and a black leather jacket, he looked like every woman's dream come true.

'Hello,' she breathed, her eyes lifting to his face, tracing over the classically chiselled features, marvelling again at the way Mother Nature had fashioned each perfect bone.

She stood there staring at him for some moments before realising that *he* was metaphorically devouring *her*. Rhea's pulse-rate soared as she saw his admiration. 'You look . . . fantastic,' he murmured. 'And smell divine.'

A wave of pleasure flooded her at his having noticed her perfume, recklessly bought with money she had put aside for a special emergency. Ironic, she conceded nervously, that her first affair was considered an emergency!

Stephen grinned at Emily over Rhea's shoulder. 'Got your night things, gorgeous Gussie?'

'Sure have!'

'Come on, then. Laura will murder me if I don't have you back there pronto. She gave me five minutes.'

They made it in record time, Rhea waiting in the car while Stephen deposited Emily and her things in the house with Laura and Mrs King. *His* idea, not hers.

'I know what mothers like you are like,' he had laughingly told her as he got out of the car. 'You spend half an hour with a whole list of dos and don'ts and spoil the kids' fun. Maisie will keep them in line, never fear. I have three strict rules for Laura when I go out of an evening. No going outside, no cheek and to bed by ten-thirty, OK?'

Rhea had nodded, aware that for once her thoughts were not for her daughter or anyone else. Selfish it might be of her, she acknowledged, but tonight was hers!

But as she waited in the car, her apprehension over the evening ahead grew. Would it turn out as she had fantasised, as Stephen had promised? Would he find her gauche and unsophisticated? Would she make an utter fool of herself?

But, more to the point, where would it all end? She had not forgotten his other women. Not by a long shot.

By the time Stephen finally reappeared on the front porch, stopping briefly to lock up, her throat was dry, her hands twisting agitatedly in her lap. With a sickening churning in her stomach she watched him practically skip down the steps, whistling as he opened the door and slid in behind the wheel.

He darted her a quick glance and stopped whistling. 'You look petrified!' he pronounced, but before she could say anything he leant across and kissed her, with shocking intimacy. 'See?' He smiled into her stunned face. 'Nothing to be frightened of. I won't eat you. Well . . .' a wicked glint flashed into those beautiful grey eyes '. . . not literally'.

Rhea's blush was automatic.

Suddenly his face was serious, with a tender yearning lighting his eyes. 'I love it when you do that,' he murmured thickly, reaching out to smooth a cool hand down her heated cheek. 'You are one special lady, Rhea Petrovic, do you know that?'

She couldn't say a word, her whole being concentrating on the way his fingers were now sliding down her throat. His eyes dropped to the rapid rise and fall of her breasts before lifting to caress her face once more. Her lips had parted slightly in an effort to gain more breath for her burning lungs, her own eyes plummeting the depths of his with an insatiable yearning.

'Hell,' he muttered, snatching his hand away from where it had almost reached her breast. He sat up straight, a returning glance half reproaching her. 'If you keep looking at me like that, woman, we won't make it out of the driveway, let alone all the way into the city!'

'Oh!' Her hands automatically flew up to cover her face.

'Hey,' Stephen drew them down, forcing her to look at him again, 'none of that, now! I was only joking. I really like the way you look at me.'

'Oh, God . . .' Rhea was all afluster, her mind revolving with a mixture of embarrassment and insecurity.

'I'm well aware, Rhea,' he said gently, 'that you don't make a habit of doing this. But please . . .' his hand returned to touch her face, tracing down her cheek and around her lips '. . . do me a favour. No more guilt, eh? It's hardly flattering to me, you know. And it's not necessary. The way you feel is perfectly natural, perfectly normal, and not in any way shameful!'

With one last reproachful glance, he fired the engine and accelerated away, leaving Rhea to stare dazedly out of the passenger window, her nerves only slightly soothed.

They had reached the freeway and been driving for quite some time before Stephen spoke again. 'Tell me about your marriage,' he asked carefully.

She glanced over at him. 'What . . . what about it?'

'Where you happy?'

Rhea was never comfortable with a deliberate lie. 'I thought so . . . at the time.'

He darted a frowning look her away. 'And now you don't?'

She frowned. 'It could have been happier.'

'In what way?'

Rhea bit her bottom lip. She really didn't want to talk about her marriage. Or Milan. She still felt upset by her recent discoveries, still felt guilty that she had married

Milan for all the wrong reasons. He had not been a bad man, and had probably deserved better than his child bride.

'I was very young when I married,' she hedged. 'Just turned eighteen and barely out of school. My husband was a good deal older . . .'

'How much older?'

'Thirty-one.'

'And your parents were happy to let you marry him at such a tender age?'

Of course they hadn't been happy—Rhea could see that now. But she had insisted, like the stubborn adolescent she was.

'My father was dead by then,' she said, 'and Mum had married again. I think she was reasonably pleased to see me settled. I . . . wasn't getting along too well with my stepfather at the time.'

'Hmm. Always a tricky situation, that, a stepfather and daughter. Needs a lot of patience and understanding, I would think.'

Rhea sighed. 'Yes. And I wasn't an easy child to live with, I'm afraid. Bill was really very good to me. I've only just realised how much . . .' Her voice trailed away, tears of regret pricking her eyes as the thought of all the times her stepfather had tried to reach her. In the end he had resorted to buying her things. A stereo, then the organ—and lessons—not to mention piles of books and clothes. If only she could go back and undo some of things she had said . . .

'Hey, they aren't tears, are they?'

They had stopped at the lights at the end of the freeway and Stephen reached over to tip her face towards him. 'I'm sorry, Rhea, I didn't mean to make you cry. Was it that bad? Your childhood?'

'No,' she whispered, his fleeting touch sending her mind back to why she was here, in this car, at this moment.

'Let me kiss you better,' he murmured, leaning over to brush his lips lightly against hers.

Her hand came up tremblingly to touch the side of his jaw, to keep him there. But he drew back, taking the hand with him and pressing her fingertips to his mouth, all the while holding her with darkly hooded eyes. 'You must put them behind you, Rhea,' he said softly. 'Your childhood, your marriage. You're a woman now, a beautiful, desirable woman . . . Live your life as you see it, without fear, without any shackles from the past.'

The blaring of horns told them the lights had gone green, but Stephen did not hurry. He gave her a last, lingering look before dropping her dazed hand and turning his attention to the road ahead.

Neither of them said another word till they reached the inner city and he turned the car sharply to drop into an underground car park.

Rhea glanced around in confusion. 'But aren't we right in the middle of the city? Isn't this an office block?'

'It surely is,' Stephen smiled as he drew to a halt in a reserved parking space. 'Mine . . . I had the top floor converted into an apartment. Come on.'

He gallantly helped her out of the low-slung car and led her over to a bank of lifts. He inserted a key into a lock under a sign that said 'Penthouse Suite' and the doors whooshed open, shutting silently behind them after they entered.

Rhea was too uptight to make any comment,

especially as it was obvious that it was a private lift, reserved for the owner of the building. She threw Stephen a troubled glance. She knew he was wealthy, but somehow being confronted by such overwhelming evidence was undermining. He was way out of her league in so many ways.

'Problems?' he asked, startling her with the way he seemed in tune with her feelings.

'I . . . I . . . No . . .'

He was frowning now. 'Sure?'

Rhea dragged up a smile. 'Sure.'

The lift whisked to a halt, the doors shooting back to reveal another door. Again Stephen inserted a key. He threw open this door and ushered her inside. Rhea put her bag down on a hall table before letting Stephen take her hand and lead her down some marble steps into a sunken lounge-room. He deposited her on a black leather sofa before moving across to the bar.

'I think we could both use a drink,' he tossed over his shoulder. 'I'll mix up something potent.'

Rhea looked around the living area in a type of chilled awe. It was breathtakingly spacious, with white shag carpet, deep sofas, subtly piped music, dusky lighting and a spectacular view, not to mention the lavishly stocked bar. She wondered how many women had been bowled over with the sheer luxury of the place.

'I can see why you don't live here with Laura,' she remarked, unable to disguise her distaste at the visual scenes her mind was evoking.

Stephen looked up sharply from where he was mixing a couple of cocktails behind the bar. 'She stayed here for a month till we moved into the house.'

Rhea flinched. Surely he hadn't . . . Not while Laura was here . . .

'No, I didn't,' he grated out, walking towards her with the two drinks in his hands. 'My God, Rhea, must you always believe the worst of me?' He shoved her glass in her hand. 'I have never taken a woman to bed in front of Laura. Never!'

She stared up at him, shaken by his repeated readings of her mind. And his anger. 'I'm sorry,' she muttered. 'It's just that . . . well, this place is rather . . .'

'What?' His gaze swept around. 'Plush? Expensive? Why not? I've worked damned hard for what I've got. But it's no orgy palace. Maybe it's your narrow, prejudiced mind that sees it that way.'

A prickle ran up Rhea's spine as she saw him drain his drink in a single swallow. Everything seemed to be going wrong. 'Stephen, I'm sorry I——'

'If my lifestyle is so reprehensible,' he cut in in clipped tones, 'then why are you here with me, Rhea?' Why not find someone supposedly respectable to sleep with? Or does the idea of going to bed with a bad boy give you an extra kick?'

She clenched her glass defensively, the blunt thrust of his words cutting her to the quick. 'That's a rotten thing to say!' she rasped.

'Why? It's the truth, isn't it?' His laughter was bitter, his eyes angry. 'You can dish it out, Rhea, but can you take it? Go on, admit that all you want is for me to——'

She slapped him, hard, drowning out the crude words. 'I wish I didn't,' she choked out, hating herself and him.

Stephen rubbed his cheek and got to his feet. 'That's

· becoming painfully obvious, my dear.'

He swung away, striding over to the bar to refill his glass, downing the drink with one gulp.

Rhea put her glass down and stood up. 'I . . . I want to go home.' Her voice sounded small, lost.

He turned slowly to face her. 'No.'

Her eyes rounded at him.

'Being a bastard, I couldn't possibly let you leave, Rhea.' He began walking leisurely towards her, his face chillingly cold. 'Certainly not without your expectations being fulfilled.'

Rhea was galvanised to the spot, apprehension and anticipation sending her mind into a chaotic whirl. She couldn't think, couldn't move. She watched him approach, somehow expecting him to grab her and kiss her, but he didn't. He stopped in front of her, his mocking gaze raking her body from top to toe before quite unexpectedly cupping her breasts with his hands.

'This *is* what you came here for, isn't it?' he derided, leisurely finding and playing with her nipples through the wool. 'Not for making love,' he went on caustically. 'Just this . . .!'

She swayed, squeezing her eyes shut against the flood of feeling that had erupted deep inside her. She knew she should knock his hands away, but she couldn't, she couldn't. It was insidious the way she wasn't able to resist. So she stood there, in her dark, erotic world, holding her breath, saying nothing, yet all the while expecting, waiting for the next barrage of insults.

But they didn't come.

When his hands dropped away her eyes fluttered open, only to find him standing there, his fists clenched tightly at his side. He looked furious. And desolate. 'I could kill you for doing this, do you know that?' he growled.

'Don't!' she choked out.

'Don't what?' he snarled.

Rhea didn't know. Her whole being was a mess. She still wanted him to take her, but she wanted something else too, something so unattainable she dared not speak of it. She looked up at him with tortured eyes. 'Don't be angry with me!'

His eyes locked harshly on to hers and suddenly, the anger drained from him, his shoulders slumping.

She moved forward, sliding her hands underneath his jacket and over his chest. 'I don't really think you're a bastard,' she said softly. This time it was *her* hand lifting to *his* mouth, *her* fingers tracing *his* lips. 'I want you, Stephen,' she urged. 'I want you now — quickly!'

He groaned, grasping her brutally by the shoulders as though he was going to push her away. Instead he dragged her against him, claiming her mouth in a kiss that was so unlike him. It was brutal and savage and wild. It punished and ravaged and obliterated till Rhea was left limp and drained.

When he pushed her back across the sofa, stripping off her black trousers with a vicious yank, she was too stunned to resist. She lay there watching dazedly as he stood over her, his hands fumbling with his belt.

Suddenly he stopped.

'What . . . what is it?' she gasped.

He groaned and turned away from her, staggering over to lean shaking against the bar. 'Get dressed,' he ordered thickly.

'Dressed?'

'Yes, dammit! Straight away!'

'But . . . don't you want to . . . to . . .?'

'For pity's sake, of course I want to!' roared Stephen. 'Now get dressed!'

Rhea did as he asked, tears coming to her eyes, tears of confusion and dismay. Why had he stopped? Why?

He must be lying about having wanted to. Lying! No man would have voluntarily stopped at that point! She must have done something wrong, something to turn him off.

'I'm dressed,' she said in a little voice.

He turned and surveyed her, anger still in his face. 'Now, Rhea Petrovic,' he announced, 'we are going to go out and have some dinner. And then . . . *then* . . . we will come back here and *make love* . . . at my leisure. *Not* quickly, and *not* at your command! Do I make myself clear?'

'Yes, Stephen,' she said meekly, though waves of a delirious joy had rocketed through her veins at his forceful words. He still wanted her. He did. He did! It had been his male ego that had stopped him.

And if some other part of her inner self thrilled to his decision not to take her in anger, she brushed the feeling aside. Of course it was only his ego, she decided logically. What other reason could there be?

An exasperated smile smoothed the frustration from his face. 'What *am* I going to do with you?' he said, shaking his head as he propelled her from the room.

CHAPTER ELEVEN

'YOU'RE not eating.'

Rhea stopped fiddling with her fork. 'I don't seem to be very hungry.'

Stephen made am impatient sound. 'I bring you to an exclusive restaurant, order you lobster and you waste it!'

'You haven't eaten much yourself,' she pointed out.

He sighed and put down his cutlery. 'True.'

There was a brief awkward silence. 'Shall we go?' he asked.

She nodded, an acute shyness descending as she waited till he settled the account.

They hardly spoke during the short taxi ride back to the unit, even their meagre conversation drying up once they were in the lift.

'You've gone quiet,' Stephen remarked as the doors opened at the penthouse.

Quiet. And nervous. And totally lacking in confidence. It was one thing to be carried away with spontaneous passion, quite another, Rhea was discovering, to deliberately plan a night of intimacy.

'Sit down,' Stephen commanded once he had shepherded her inside and closed the door.

She sank into the large black sofa, watching nervously as Stephen moved behind the bar.

'This time tell me what you like,' he said, rather ambiguously.

Rhea gulped down the lump in her throat. 'Vodka and orange.' She had never had one before.

'Easy or heavy on the vodka?'

'What do you suggest?'

He lifted one eyebrow in a dry fashion. 'Heavy, by the look of you.'

She laughed, and it eased some of her tension. 'OK . . . heavy.'

He was very adept at the mixing of her drink, and she remembered how he had once said he was good at a lot of things. She believed him.

'Aren't you having anything?' she quizzed when he came over with only the one glass.

Stephen smiled, shaking his head as he handed the drink over and sat down next to her. 'Alcohol is a good relaxant for women,' he commented quite naturally, 'but a poor aphrodisiac for men.'

Rhea coloured.

'You blush beautifully,' he murmured, one of his arms sliding along the back of the sofa to play with the hair on her shoulders. 'But I've told you that, haven't I?'

She felt even hotter but lifted a defiant chin. 'I think you like to embarrass me.'

His eyes teased her. 'You could be right. I have to pay you back somehow.'

She frowned. 'Pay me back?'

He gave her the oddest look. It was both sardonic and sad, pricking at her conscience. Though why, she didn't know. Men like Stephen Chase were invulnerable.

Rhea lifted the drink to her lips, holding his gaze over the rim of the glass, reminding herself every time her heart lurched of all the women he had used and discarded over the years.

'Sometimes I wonder what goes on in that pretty little

head of yours,' he said.

She gave another nervous laugh. 'You seem to be able to read my mind very well!'

'Only in some matters.'

'And what am I thinking now?' she challenged, taking several more sips of the potent drink.

'God only knows ... Women's minds can be the ultimate mystery. They often say one thing and mean another.'

'Is that why you've never married one?' she asked, and took a bigger swallow.

'Not at all,' Stephen answered with a laugh. 'I adore female company, but I realised quite early on that I couldn't work the hours I did and keep a family happy at the same time. It was as simple as that.'

She took another sip, trying to control a surge of irritation at the offhandedness of his reply. 'Did you come to this *simple* decision before or after you met Laura's mother?' came her caustic query. 'Maybe she didn't tell you she was pregnant because she knew your feelings on the subject of marriage and family.'

He stared at her for a moment, then leant over and lifted the glass from her hand. 'I think perhaps we'll dispense with this,' he muttered, putting it down on a side-table with a thump. 'You seem to be one of those aggressive drinkers.'

'Don't be ridic——'

'Hush!' he whispered, placing three fingers against her lips. 'Don't spoil things.' The fingers moved lightly over her lips, then down to her throat.

Rhea was instantly spellbound, any annoyance dissolving as she became caught up in the shivery feelings his feathery touch was producing. He traced the neckline of her top, making her gasp when he dipped into the valley between her breasts. The thought that he was going to touch her breasts, to stroke and fondle them, had her holding her breath in dizzy expectation, but instead that tantalising hand reached up to brush her hair back on one side.

'Lovely hair . . . Lovely ear . . .' Even now a fingertip was encircling its outer shell, breaking her skin out into goose-bumps.

'Stop it!' she shuddered, but made no attempt to strike his hand away.

'Why?' The grey eyes mocked her.

'Because . . .'

'Come now, you like it. You don't really want me to stop, do you?' Stephen leant forward to replace his fingers with his mouth. 'Do you?' he breathed into the ear.

'No,' she shivered.

He sat up straight, his face almost world-weary. 'Then close your eyes and enjoy it, Rhea. We haven't got all night.'

For a few appalled moments she could only stare at him, his attitude throwing her, but then her eyes were closing and he was tipping her back till her head rested against the soft sofa. She sensed rather than saw his face loom over hers, her whole body stiff with anticipation.

'When I kiss you,' he murmured against her lips, 'I want you to relax. Give yourself up to me—totally.'

She made some sort of sound, like the quivering cry of a frightened animal.

'Relax, Rhea . . .'

His lips were so soft on hers she didn't realise they were there for a moment. But then they moved, sensuously, rubbing across hers in a side-to-side movement till her mouth tingled with sensitivity. 'So sweet,' he whispered. 'So incredibly sweet . . .'

Then it was his tongue moving over her lips, moistening them with warm licking movements, sending hot jabs of sensation darting through her brain. She groaned when he drew back slightly, the air cooling her heated lips, making her even more aware of their pouting swollen state.

But his desertion was only brief. This time the kiss was deeper, his tongue penetrating into her mouth, sliding down beside hers into the warm depths. Rhea's body leapt in response, blood racing in heated cirles in her head. Her shoulders lifted from the sofa as she strained to be closer to him, for while their mouths were fused, no other part of their bodies were touching. She wanted—no, *needed*—more physical contact.

Unexpectedly, one of his hands slid up under her top, capturing a single breast, the weight of his possession pushing her back. She gasped with delight and shock, shivers running up and down her spine as his hand moved, stroking the tip into a taut tight bud of bursting sensation.

Her heart seemed to suspend its beat in her chest till in the end she grew light-headed from lack of air. She tried to twist her head away, but in vain, for his other hand had moved to firmly cup the back of her head, keeping her mouth captive beneath his.

The kiss went on and on, the hand on her breast arousing her still further with its sensuous explorations till a swirling blackness hovered at the edges of her mind.

Finally, terrified she might lose consciousness, she burst from his mouth. 'Stephen!' she gasped.

'Yes?'

She was shocked by the coolness in his voice, the complete control he appeared to have over his emotions.

'I . . . I . . .'

He cupped her face with steady hands. 'You what?' he murmured, his annoyingly passive gaze searching hers.

'Oh, God,' she moaned, knowing that she was definitely out of her depth here, with this man. The butterfly had been well and truly pinned.

'Let me take this off,' he suggested, plucking casually at one of the sleeves of her top.

'No!'

He reproached her silently with a look.

A surge of rebellious anger sent her sitting upright, whipping the scarlet top over her head and flinging it to the floor. 'Satisfied?' she threw at him.

Lazy grey eyes flicked over the full, rosy-tipped curves. 'Infinitely,' he drawled, and his head began to descend.

She watched, astonished, fascinated, as his mouth drew closer, holding her breath in an agony of apprehension and anticipation. When the parted lips closed over one aching point, the breath was punched from her body. Her chest heaved, grew still, then heaved again as she dragged in several gasping, life-saving breaths.

'Don't . . . Oh, don't!' she whimpered, barely able to stand the pleasure-pain of his attentions. But he went on, tugging a nipple into his mouth, nipping it gently with his teeth, licking it with his tongue, then releasing it to the sting of the air before beginning again.

Rhea's head dropped back on to the sofa, her mouth falling open, her eyes wildly dilated. Her flesh pulsated, ached, pleaded to be soothed and stroked.

Only gradually did she realise that the pleading was not silent. 'Oh, please . . . Stephen, please!' she begged in a voice she scarcely recognised.

Suddenly she was abandoned, her glazed eyes opening to find him standing up looking down at her. Still, amazingly, he seemed unaffected. 'I want you to undress me,' he said, the thick harshness of his voice betraying that perhaps his composure was a sham, that to appear calm he was actually exercising an enormous control over himself.

Trembling, Rhea pulled herself upright, then stood up, her face flaming as she remembered her semi-nakedness. 'Right here?' she rasped. 'With . . . with the light on?'

'Yes.'

An unnerving panic at her own lack of experience made her hesitate, but he waited patiently, watching her through half-closed eyes. Finally her hands lifted, shaking as she pushed the leather jacket from his shoulders, unable to catch it as it fell to the floor.

'Leave it!' he growled.

Then, with tremulous fingers, she started on the buttons of his shirt. All the time he was staring at her, holding her with that sensuous, hooded gaze.

She stopped at the last button, loath to proceed, to expose his magnificent male chest. For he *was* magnificent, a perfect specimen of masculine symmetry, broad where necessary, tapering down to a lean, tight hardness.

It had been one of her fantasies, to have him invite her touch. Yet now it was all too frighteningly real. She wasn't sure how she would react or cope once she let her hands loose on him.

'Something wrong?' he muttered.

'No . . . It's just that . . .'

'Don't you want to touch me?' Cynical eyes taunted her. 'Is this another of your little games, Rhea?'

A surge of anger exploded inside her head and she ripped the shirt asunder, paling afterwards at the shock of what she had done. But he only laughed, a low, sexy sound, shrugging off the torn garment and throwing it aside.

'I often wondered what you were hiding behind that prim exterior of yours, my lovely Rhea. Now I know,' He snatched up her hands, spreading her palms against his chest, holding her wrists. 'Touch me, Rhea . . . touch me properly,' he demanded, the fever in his eyes at last reassuring her that he was as aroused as she was.

She gazed back at him, wanting to explore him oh, so badly, but still feeling awkward, foolish.

'Like this . . .' He moved her hands over his skin, down across his ribcage, then back up through the soft curls in the centre of his chest.

His hands dropped away, but his half-closed eyes held her, their smoky sensuality inviting her, exciting her.

Her fingers moved, slowly, tentatively, tracing across his male muscles like a sculptor lovingly modelling clay. How smooth he felt, smooth and warm and strong, like corded velvet wrapped around steel.

She grew bolder, moulding the muscles as she went, feeling and kneading with a growing sense of awe at the way he was responding to her touch. His breathing had quickened into deep ragged bursts. His eyes flashed with incandescent lights whenever her palms inadvertently grazed across his male nipples.

'Enough!' he barked at last, yanking her roughly against him, rubbing her naked breasts against him with vigorous, tortured movements. Then abruptly he swept her up into his arms, striding into the bedroom, where he dropped her on a king-sized bed, yanking off her shoes, then stripping her totally naked.

'The light!' she gasped, her face turning away as he stared down at her spread-eagled nudity.

Again he laughed. 'I want to see you, Rhea. All of you!'

She lay there, riveted by his smouldering gaze, watching breathlessly as he began to undo his belt. But despite her arousal, despite her desperate longing for him, she was horribly nervous. What if it was a disaster, after all? What if they were both left disappointed?

'Stephen, I . . .' She stopped as he unzipped, then stepped out of his trousers. 'I . . .' Any protest died in her throat as he discarded his underpants.

'It's . . . been a long time,' she whispered hoarsely at last.

He joined her on the bed, leaning over her to kiss her with tender understanding. 'I know,' he murmured.

'But I have to tell you, I'm not . . .' she turned her face to one side '. . . not very good at this.'

He turned her face back with a gentle hand, making her look up at him. 'Who on earth told you that?' he soothed. 'My God, Rhea, you're the most responsive, the most sensual woman I've ever known!' He ran a fingertip lightly over one breast, making her quiver with pleasure. 'See?'

All she could see was that it was *his* skill, not hers. 'I

. . . I'm not usually like this.' She shivered. 'You make me feel things, Stephen. You . . . Oh!' she moaned as he began to lazily encircle her nipple. 'Don't . . .'

He stopped, bringing a wide-eyed pleading glance from Rhea. Of course she hadn't really meant him to stop. It was just that the intense feelings his touch produced sometimes frightened her.

There was something oddly sad in his smile. 'You really must stop doing that—saying no when you mean yes.'

'But I——'

He placed a restraining finger on her lips. 'Hush! I understand—really I do. Better than you think. It's just that . . . Oh, hell, I might as well be noble just this once . . .'

His kiss was heartbreakingly tender, tasting her lips, tempting her with the withholding of his tongue till she whimpered, opening her mouth wider, sending her own tongue forward to invite his. He complied with a hoarse moan.

Time after time, Rhea's senses were to be shocked, then soothed, excited and extended. Stephen kissed her where she had never been kissed before, touched and explored with a bold breathless intimacy that left her quivering with expectation and wonder. Nothing he did to her seemed wrong. Nothing. He gave her pleasure such as she had never experienced, or even fantasised about, gave and gave and gave till she was teetering on an unknown brink, gripped by an unbearable tension that demanded a release that till now had remained a mystery to her.

She began to tremble, to cry, to feel helpless,

hopeless, frightened.

He stopped.

Her groan carried anguish, and sheer frustration.

He stroked her face. 'Soon, darling, soon,' he murmured, holding and caressing her till her breathing steadied and she lay pliant and relaxed in his arms. Then quietly, with an incredible gentleness, he moved over her, filling her with his strong, awe-inspiring virility, taking her breath away.

'Oh, Stephen!' she sighed.

Wonderful, he had said it would be. Rhea would have chosen another word: overwhelming.

It overwhelmed her. *He* overwhelmed her, slowly at first, then surging powerfully till every nerve-ending in her body was throbbing with an unbelievable pleasure. Swiftly and silently she soared, higher and higher than before, heart beating, head whirling, on and on till with a burst of bliss everything shattered around her and she was catapulted headlong into another dimension. And while she was still being consumed by this incredible ecstasy, she heard him cry out, felt his shuddering climax.

Then she was clinging to him, holding him tight, telling him he was wonderful, confessing that she had never felt anything like that before. Never! All the while trying to stop the tears from coming.

And if, in the deepest corners of her soul, that secret wish stirred again, she tried to ignore it, steadfastly telling herself that she had gone into this with her eyes open, and not to expect more than was offered. Sex was all there would be with a man like Stephen. He would never offer more.

He sighed, lifting his head from her breasts to look at

her briefly, then he sank back down, his lips grazing a still sensitised point. She shuddered.

'Don't move,' he commanded softly. 'I need to rest for a few minutes.'

Rhea closed her eyes, willing herself not to think or worry, but to just lie there and enjoy the feeling of the moment, the way her body was floating down, down, relaxing, melting. Contentment was spreading, as was an insidious desire to sleep. Eventually she sighed, her body shifting slightly under his.

'Hush, my darling,' he murmured. 'Hush now. Go to sleep—rest. It's over.' And he pulled the quilt around them, the warmth embracing her, his hands and voice calming her till she was lying still and silent.

Rest, she told herself. Rest . . .

But she couldn't rest, couldn't sleep. She lay there, eyes wide, listening as Stephen's breathing gradually became deep and even, his arms heavy upon her. The tears had dried on her cheeks, but her soul was crying as it tried to come to terms with his last word.

Over . . . Over . . . Over . . .

She didn't want it to be over. She didn't want it *ever* to be over! She wanted Stephen now, even more than before. She wanted him in her heart as well as her body. She wanted him in her life, her thoughts, her every breath.

With a groan she turned her face into his chest, pressing her lips to his flesh. He stirred slightly, his arms instinctively moving around her, but remained asleep.

'Oh, Stephen,' she cried softly in the dark, 'I've fallen in love with you . . . I have been all along. Whatever am I going to do?'

CHAPTER TWELVE

'RHEA!'

She shot awake with a gasp to find Stephen fully dressed standing over her, shaking her shoulder.

'It's almost seven,' he explained.

Her mouth gaped. 'Almost *seven*! Oh, heavens, why didn't you . . . ?' She went to jump up, remembered her naked state and groaned, clutching the quilt defensively. Panic at the situation crowded all other thoughts from her mind.

'Don't worry,' he went on, calmly seating himself on the edge of the bed. 'I rang Maisie and explained that we'd stayed in town rather than drive all the way home through the Saturday night traffic. She said the girls were still asleep, so I told her not to say anything about my not coming home, to let them think I was already up and down the road buying the Sunday papers if they awoke. Still, I think we'd better get a move on.'

Rhea had stared at him in appalled silence during this speech. The words came out so smoothly, the excuses sounding depressingly practised.

Which of course was perfectly understandable. 'Mornings after' were an everyday occurrence for him, not a once-in-a-lifetime happening. It brought home to her even more forcibly how stupid she was to have let herself fall in love with him.

Yet despite her dismay Rhea suddenly found herself looking at his mouth, his hands, his body. A telling heat spread through her as memories flooded her mind, and she bit her lip in shy embarrassment, dropping her eyes to the floor.

Stephen sighed, and got to his feet. 'The en-suite's in there. Coffee and toast in ten minutes.'

The shower, the getting dressed, the hurried breakfast, the drive home, were all agony. Rhea couldn't bear to look at Stephen, let alone talk to him, so the time passed in a series of unbearable silences.

But she had to speak once they turned from the main highway on to the road that would lead to Bangaloo Creek.

'Please, Stephen,' she whispered in a tight, hoarse voice, 'don't roar down my street like you usually do. 'I . . . don't want . . .'

'. . . the neighbours to hear,' he finished for her, his words clipped and curt.

'Yes . . .' She hung her head, knowing he thought her an unsophisticated bore.

'I don't think they would really care, do you?' he said wearily. 'But I'll do my best not to embarrass you, Rhea. I also think it wise that we don't see each other again—at least not on a personal basis. I do realise we can hardly avoid each other completely.'

Her eyes flew to him, pain filling her face. 'But *why*?'

His sidewards glance was astonishingly bitter. 'Let's just say I don't fancy playing stud for a woman who doesn't like or respect me as a man.'

Rhea's mouth opened, then snapped shut. Playing stud? Was that how he saw last night? She struggled to see the evening from his point of view, finally conceding that it might have appeared she was using his body merely to service her needs. He wouldn't understand that she had pushed aside all her other feelings for him to focus on the sex, because she thought that was all she could have.

But she knew now that her feelings for him went far deeper than physical desire. And it wasn't true that she didn't like or respect him. She liked and admired him tremendously. She admired the way he had taken on his responsibility regarding Laura. She admired his intelligence and self-assurance. She certainly admired his capacity for being sensitive and gentle. If only she could explain that she had been overly critical about his bachelor lifestyle because she was falling in love with him, and wanted him to be different in his attitude towards women and marriage!

But how could she do that? He didn't love her back, and it would seem as if she was begging him to stay with her. He would probably accuse her of using emotional blackmail to get what she wanted from him. It reminded her of that phone call from Madeline . . .

Rhea groaned. Thinking of Madeline brought a rush of new thoughts. Perhaps Stephen's excuse for leaving his relationship with her at a one-night stand was just that—an excuse. Maybe he wanted to drop her because she'd disappointed him in bed. Maybe he liked his partners to be far more uninhibited, far more adventurous.

Rhea cringed as she thought he might have found her boring. She glanced across at him, but he wasn't looking at her. He was staring straight ahead, his jaw jutting forward with cold resolution.

A black pit yawned in her soul. It was useless, she realised. Useless . . . It *was* over.

Her eyes closed, tears hovering.

Stephen turned the car into her road very carefully, putting the gears into neutral and gliding silently down the hill, where he swung into her driveway, coming to a halt with only the barest noise. 'I'm afraid I might not be able to leave as quietly,' he muttered, 'but I'll do my best.'

Rhea turned her face away while she got the tears under control, the atmosphere one of strained silence.

'You'd better go inside,' he said at last, his tone brusque. 'I'll drop Emily off after lunch.'

'Thank you.' She went to open the door, her heart breaking, and suddenly she couldn't do it, couldn't let him go without telling him something of how she felt. 'Stephen, I——'

'For God's sake, Rhea,' he cut in brutally, 'don't make polite conversation now! Your silence this morning said more than enough, believe me.' He twisted to fully face her in the car, his expression one of controlled anger. 'Be honest, darling! You needed a man, probably have done for six years. I just happened to be the poor lad you finally chose to work out your frustrations on. Fair enough—I can accept that. Hell, I did, didn't I? But the least you could have done was look me in the eye this morning and say thank you, Stephen, I enjoyed it, Stephen, not slink out of my place as if you were a fallen woman!'

He leant across her, unsnapped her seatbelt and pushed open the door. 'Now be a good girl and run along. And next time, Rhea, find someone you actually *like* as your lover, then he won't mind coming back for seconds!'

Complete humiliation had her scrambling from the car and literally running up the path. As she fumbled with her key, she heard the car reverse out and drive off.

She stumbled inside, Stephen's crippling taunts whirling through her mind. Did he have to be so hard, so cruel? OK, so she had probably been wrong, selfishly taking the pleasure his body could give her because she knew that was all of him she would ever get. But did he have to throw her inexperience, her feelings of shame in her face?

With a sob, she slumped down in a chair at the kitchen table, her head falling into her hands as she burst into tears. 'Bastard!' she cried. 'Bastard . . .'

Bobby came into the kitchen and whimpered at her ankles till Rhea bent down and scratched his ears, the sobs slowly receding. 'Miss me?' she asked the dog.

Bobby sat and whimpered some more.

Something niggled at Rhea's memory and she sat upright, dashing the dampness from her cheeks. 'Where's Dolly?' she asked with a frown.

Another whimper.

Rhea stood up, a sickening sensation claiming her stomach. What was it Emily had said the night before? Something about the dogs not being there when she brought the food? That was not like them, particularly not like Dolly . . .

'Oh, no!' Rhea groaned, and was already up and running.

She dashed out to the kennel, fearing what she would find. But it was worse than she had imagined. Two tiny dead puppies lay in the straw, and Dolly . . . Dolly was lying with terrifying stillness in one corner.

Rhea crashed to her knees, her face white. 'Oh, please God, no, I couldn't bear it!' she gasped, trembling fingers running over the small bundle. Suddenly Dolly made a sound, opening her eyes and looking at Rhea with intolerable pain. Rhea rocked back, at once relieved yet distressed at witnessing such agony.

'It's all right, Dolly,' she soothed, stroking the now shivering animal with infinite tenderness. 'I'm here now, I'll get help—you'll be all right. Mummy's here . . .' She went to leave, but Dolly made a sound, a whimpering plea for the solace of her owner's presence. Yet Rhea knew she had to get a vet. And fast.

A decision had to be made. As slowly and as gently as she could, she scooped the dog up into her arms, carrying her into the house. There she wrapped her in a rug, holding her with one arm as she looked up the number and dialled the vet, the receiver tucked under her chin.

'Is the vet there? Oh, it's you, Margaret. It's Rhea Petrovic here . . . My dog's in trouble. She's having pups and a couple have been stillborn. She's in awful pain, and I wondered . . . He can't come? Operating . . . Bring the dog round. All right, I'm on my way.'

She hung up. It wasn't far, she reasoned, trying to keep herself calm. Only a couple of miles. It wouldn't take long . . .

She didn't bother to lock up, carrying the dog out to the old van and laying her gently on the front seat. Dolly was moaning softly, the sound cutting through Rhea's heart. She inserted the key with a trembling hand, all the while looking anxiously at the dog. She turned the ignition.

It wouldn't start. The rotten old thing wouldn't start!

Rhea could not believe it. Ancient it might be, but it usually started. This time it didn't.

She swore and thumped the wheel, trying the ignition again and again in panic until of course the battery was totally dead.

For a moment she couldn't think, her head sinking down on to the wheel. Then suddenly she grew aware that Dolly was not making any sound. She leant over and touched her, but there was no response. 'No!' she cried, sweeping the little dog up and racing inside, stumbling over a bewildered Bobby as she went. Desperate fingers found the right numbers as if by some miracle.

'Stephen Chase here.'

'Oh, Stephen,' she sobbed, her eyes awash, 'it's Dolly! She had her pups last night and she's . . . I think she's dying . . . I rang the vet, but . . . but he couldn't come . . . He's operating. He said to bring her, but the van wouldn't start . . . Oh, please come, Stephen! I need you . . .'

'I'll be right there.'

She found herself standing there, staring into the dead receiver. Only then did she realise what she had done. In her desperation and need she had automatically turned to the man she loved, the man she had just called a bastard.

And what had he done? He'd asked no questions, given no excuses, wasted no time. He was coming straight away, answering her plea without any thought of retaliation for the way he believed she had treated him.

Rhea frowned, baffled by his behaviour. Could she be terribly wrong about him? About everything?

Bobby whimpered at her feet, bringing her thoughts back to the little dog in her arms. 'Oh, Dolly,' she cried, 'you have to get well! You just have to!' And she went outside to wait for Stephen.

This time he made no attempt to arrive quietly. He roared down the road in an arrival reminiscent of his first, careering across the culvert of the driveway with no heed to life or limb.

Rhea ran up to the car. 'Don't get out.' She climbed in, throwing him a grateful look. 'It was good of you to come so quickly. In fact, it was good of you to come at all ...'

His mouth thinned. 'You didn't think I'd let an innocent dog die, did you?' He glared at her. 'Perhaps you would,' he muttered, reversing out of the drive with a sudden burst. 'You don't have to give me directions—I know where the veterinary hospital is.'

They screeched off at a hair-raising speed, with Rhea grateful that there was little traffic early on a Sunday morning. 'Emily!' she blurted out as they swung round the first corner. 'You didn't tell her about Dolly, did you?'

'Of course not! What do you take me for? Don't answer that! Anyway, neither of the girls have surfaced yet. Look, shut up, will you, and let me concentrate on getting that dog of yours and us safely to the hospital? These roads are disgusting!'

Rhea bit her lip and glanced down at the limp little body in her arms. An overwhelming guilt swamped her and she began to cry softly, torturing herself with the thought that if she hadn't been so wrapped up in her own selfish desires the evening before she would have noticed something was wrong with Dolly. Knowing now that she loved Stephen didn't make her feel any less guilty. It was all her fault—Dolly's condition, Stephen's obvious contempt, the whole rotten mess her life was in!

Sobs, deep and wretched, racked her body.

Stephen muttered something under his breath and drove even faster.

The vet's wife, Margaret, was watching for her, coming out to meet the car as it pulled up. 'Sorry we couldn't come to you,' she apologised, opening the passenger door and taking Dolly from a teary Rhea. 'Richard's just finishing with the other op. Hmm . . . looks bad, but she's still alive. And dogs are incredibly resilient. Do you want to wait?' she asked kindly.

'Yes,' husked Rhea.

'Right—I'll be a while. Richard's nurse isn't on duty this early on a Sunday, so I have to help.'

'We'll wait out here in the car,' Stephen said.

The woman hurried off, all efficiency and business.

Rhea let out a trembling sigh, sinking back into the seat. 'If Dolly dies,' she whispered shakily, 'I'll never forgive myself. Never!'

'Rhea,' Stephen said tautly, 'this could have happened any time, while you were anywhere, not necessarily . . .'

The unspoken words hovered in the air. Not necessarily cavorting all night in bed, thinking of no one but yourself . . .

'No, it *is* my fault,' she confessed. 'There were signs, symptoms, but I failed to notice them because I was too caught up with . . .' She made a choking sound and turned her face away, guilt again overwhelming her.

'You're being too hard on yourself, Rhea,' he insisted. 'We all make mistakes.'

She groaned. 'And the biggest was last night.'

Stephen sighed and fell silent. Time dragged on.

An hour later the vet made an appearance, startling Rhea at the open passenger window. She had been sitting in the car with her eyes closed.

'Well, Rhea? You have one very sick little dog there. I've done all I can. She had a extra large pup left inside, blocking her passage in the breach position. I'm afraid I couldn't save it. But the mother's hanging on, and I believe you have reason to hope. Tough little beasts, these terriers. They cling to life just like they cling to everything else, the devils.'

He tapped Rhea on the arm. 'Now, no more tears . . .' But even as he spoke tears were swimming in his own eyes. He coughed. 'You women and your pets,' he said gruffly. 'Now off you go home . . . ring me after lunch.'

He swung away, striding back into the building, leaving Rhea feeling drained, and only mildly hopeful. Somehow she felt fate did not mean to deal her a kind hand over this. Fate wanted to punish her for her wicked selfishness.

Stephen started the car in silence, driving home slowly and without saying a word. Once they had pulled up in the drive, he alighted, helping a limp Rhea from her seat in true gentlemanly fashion. 'Do you want me to stay with you?' he asked softly.

She glanced up at him, trying to see what lay behind those inscrutable grey eyes. Was he just being kind in a neighbourly fashion? Or did he still have some feeling left for her? He had liked her once, she was sure of that. Liked and desired. She doubted if much of either remained now.

He shook his head at her failure to answer him, the gesture betraying a regret that he had even offered in the first place. 'I'll keep Emily with me for the day,' he said. 'I'll tell her I organised it with you last night, that you wanted to sleep in today.'

Rhea nodded a weary agreement, no longer amazed by his generosity of spirit. She had always known he could be kind.

'No reason to upset the girls yet,' he went on. 'Besides, you might have good news later.'

Good news . . . Rhea almost laughed. Even if Dolly lived, damage had been done, innocent people had been hurt. 'I was going to buy her a pony,' she murmured, more to herself than to Stephen. 'Emily always wanted a pony . . .'

The tears flooded back and she turned to walk away.

Stephen's hand closed over her shoulder, staying her. 'Rhea . . .' She glanced up at him through soggy lashes. 'I don't like to see you upset like this.'

'Don't you think I deserve it?' she croaked.

He didn't answer, a deep frown creasing his forehead. Rhea shook her head, turned and walked away.

CHAPTER THIRTEEN

DOLLY lived.

It was touch and go for quite some time, but in the end she survived, perhaps even better than Bobby. The poor little dog spent the entire time of Dolly's stay in hospital in a bleak depression, moping about with a long face, not eating a scrap. He grew so thin, Rhea began to worry.

But it was a different picture when Rhea brought Dolly home on the Saturday morning two weeks later. 'Out you go,' she said, opening the door of the patched-up van for Dolly to jump down.

The two dogs were instantly all over each other like a rash, Bobby's little eyes lighting up with joy. He leapt around in delighted circles, his stumpy tail going fifty to the dozen.

'He sure missed Dolly, didn't he, Mum?' Emily said.

Rhea sighed. 'Yes, he sure did . . .'

As *she* was missing Stephen. He hadn't called, not since he had brought Emily home that Sunday night. But Rhea hadn't really expected him to.

'Grandma rang while you were getting Dolly,' Emily said. 'She wants us to come down tomorrow for the day. I said you'd ring back.'

Rhea sighed. She didn't feel up to driving all that way. She went inside, picked up the phone, and dialled.

'Mum? Yes, Emily told me . . . Dolly's fine . . . Well, it's like this, Mum. I'm feeling awfully tired and . . .' She stopped, having unexpectedly seen her reflection in the kitchen dresser. How awful she was looking, thin and drawn. She hadn't been eating much. Just like Bobby.

'Mum? I've changed my mind,' she said. 'I'd love to come. Only one thing . . . I'm bringing the dogs.'

Rhea perked up immediately, now the decision had been made. Besides, she had been wanting an opportunity to give something to Bill, just some small gift to show how much she wanted their relationship to be closer. But what? Clothes were out of the question as she wasn't sure of his sizes.

In the end she bought him a carton of his favourite beer. It put a hole in the next week's housekeeping, but what the heck? Bill was worth it!

She would always remember the look on his face when she gave it to him the next day. He had difficulty stammering out his shocked 'thank you'. Rhea had the sneaky suspicion that his bending to pat the dogs at that moment was so he could surreptitiously blink away a tear or two, for when he straightened up again his eyes were suspiciously damp.

'That was a sweet thing you did for Bill, Rhea,' her mother commented as soon as they were alone. They were sitting on the beach under the umbrella. Bill and Emily and the dogs had gone for a walk along the sand looking for shells. 'I know you don't have much money.'

Rhea shrugged. 'We manage OK.'

'Bill was surprised.' Her mother's face showed she was surprised too.

'I know,' Rhea murmured, a lump forming in her throat. 'I . . . I wanted to make it up to him for being such a bitch all these years.'

'But, Rhea, you haven't been any such thing! My dear, don't ever think that. Bill understood—we both did—how you must have felt when we got married so soon after your father's death. I particularly felt guilty because it seemed disloyal to your father's memory, but I . . . I couldn't seem to help myself, love. I fell in love with Bill and I . . . we . . . I didn't want the neighbours sniggering behind your back, so we got married. I know we should have waited longer, but . . .'

Rhea could hear the guilt in her mother's words, and it reminded her forcibly of how she had felt about feeling passion for Stephen, as though it were wrong to feel that way. But of course it wasn't wrong, and especially not wrong if one was in love!

'You did the right thing, Mum,' she said gently. 'You deserved to be happy. It couldn't have been easy living with a man like Dad.'

Her mother's face snapped up, her eyes rounding.

'I've grown up, Mum,' Rhea went on with a reassuring smile. 'I don't see things with adolescent eyes any more.'

Her mother was truly taken aback. 'Bill is so different from your father,' she explained haltingly. 'He wants me as a woman, not as a wife or mother or housekeeper. He makes me feel beautiful. I did love your father, Rhea—I did! But not in the same way I love Bill.'

Rhea's heart went out to her mother's distress, for she knew exactly what she was feeling. 'Please don't feel guilty any more, Mum,' she said, hugging her. 'The love you and Bill share is very special. And it doesn't belittle what you felt for Dad. It's just . . . different. Better.'

'Oh, Rhea, it's so good to hear you talk like this. I never thought you would understand.' Her mother drew back and dabbed at her eyes, then gave her daughter a closer look, a frown crossing her face. 'You know, Rhea, you don't look all that well.'

Rhea sighed. 'I haven't been the best,' she admitted.

'Is that why you gave up playing the organ? Emily told me you'd cancelled all your engagements.'

'I suppose so . . .' In truth she couldn't bear the thought of playing music at weddings for a while.

'Is it a virus? Have you been to the doctor?'

An odd little laugh came to her lips. She pictured herself going to the doctor and describing her virus. It was a new strain, called 'Stephenitis'.

Rhea glanced up at her mother and was taken aback at the depth of concern she saw there. With her newly enlightened eyes she realised that the woman next to her felt about her the same way she felt about Emily. Rhea had never thought about her own mother's love in that light before. But it paved the way to her being more open, more frank than had been her custom.

'It's a man, Mum,' she found herself saying.

It was her mother's turn for astonishment. 'A man?'

Rhea smiled softly. 'Is that so strange?'

'No, I . . . well, you've always been a bit . . .'

'Anti-men? Frigid?'

'Well, I wouldn't say that, exactly. But you did seem . . . withdrawn. I often wondered if Milan had been . . . well . . . kind to you.'

Rhea was amazed. 'What on earth do you mean?'

Her mother scrunched up her face in agitation. 'Don't

take me the wrong way—I don't mean he'd beaten you or anything, but to be honest, Rhea, I could never take to that man. He was far too possessive, far too rigid in his ways. Chauvinistic too. He seemed to regard you as a prized possession, not a person with feelings. He . . . he reminded me of your father.'

Rhea sighed. 'I've come to the same conclusion. But only recently. I guess till I met Stephen I didn't know any better.'

'And it's this Stephen who's opened your eyes?'

Rhea nodded.

'Tell me about him, love. Is it serious between you and him?'

Serious? Was going to bed with a man serious these days? Rhea shrugged. 'If you mean have I slept with him, then yes, I have. But it's over now. He doesn't want to see me any more.'

'But you love him?'

'Yes, I love him.'

'I see . . . Why don't you tell me about him?'

Rhea did, leaving out nothing, even to baring the unbearable words Stephen had flung at her that ghastly morning.

'So you see, Mum?' she finished. 'He doesn't want anything more to do with me. And I can understand that. The man does have his pride. Not to mention Madeline and who knows how many other women?' she finished bitterly.

'But can't you see he really liked you, Rhea? More than liked, I would say. And you don't know for sure that he's still seeing these other women, do you?'

Rhea frowned. 'No . . . No, I suppose not.'

'Oh, Rhea, don't cut off your nose to spite your face. If you really love this man then fight for him. Go to him, tell him how you feel.'

'Oh, no, I couldn't!' Rhea protested.

'Why not?'

'Because I . . . I . . . because he doesn't love me!'

'How do you know?' asked her mother.

'Well, if he did he would have told me!'

'Would he?' her mother inserted gently. 'The same way you told him, I suppose?'

Rhea gasped, a thousand tiny hopes springing into life. She tried to dampen them down, tried to stop them from sweeping aside all the facts as she knew them. How could she dismiss the girl in the coffee lounge, Madeline, Laura's mother, not to mention all the others she had never seen or heard of? Stephen was a lover of the female sex, not a lover of love.

'Rhea?' her mother cut into her thoughts. 'Do you love this man or don't you?'

She nodded again.

'Well, then? What have you got to lose?'

Rhea turned to stare at her mother, her luminescent blue eyes showing that hope had won at last.

'Yes, my darling . . . go to him! Tell him how you feel. At least give yourself a chance of happiness.'

CHAPTER FOURTEEN

RHEA glanced up at the office block, not recognising it from street level, but knowing it was the right one. 'Chase Investments' was engraved in bold black letters above the glass doors.

'Mr Chase has gone into his office,' Maisie had told Rhea when she had called at Stephen's house. 'He won't be back tonight either. He's working late and will stay the night in the penthouse.'

'Oh!' Rhea's face had fallen. She had never imagined he would be working on a Sunday afternoon.

'Why don't you drive in and see him, dear?' Maisie was no fool and she could see Rhea was dressed up to the nines, in full make-up and wearing the blue silk dress Stephen had once admired. 'I'm sure he could do with a break—he's been working non-stop for days on end. I'll mind Emily for you.'

Rhea had said thank you but that Emily was staying with her grandmother for a couple of days in Kiama. Maisie gave her Stephen's office address, assuring her that there would be someone to let her into the building. Rhea had almost backed out at that stage, but somehow found herself parking the van at the nearest railway station and catching a train into Sydney's Central Station.

Now here she was, hovering nervously on the pavement, thinking she was a fool to believe her life could be sorted out by the simple admission of, 'I love you, Stephen.' Even if Stephen did care for her, he was not a marrying man. He had already stated his views on that matter.

What would he ever offer her except a few hours here, a night there? Deep in her heart Rhea desperately wanted much more than that. She wanted to marry him, to share his life, to make a family with himself and Laura and Emily. But she knew, deep down, that was only a pipe-dream.

Anguish pressed into her heart and mind, and she almost turned away. Almost . . .

But she couldn't. She realised that now. She couldn't turn her back on trying to secure for herself even the smallest part of Stephen's life. If she didn't, she would be utterly miserable anyway. Better that Emily should have a mother who was at least happy sometimes. An hour, a day, a minute with Stephen was preferable to a lifetime without him, whether he loved her or not!

The glass doors of the building were locked, but Rhea could see a security guard sitting at the reception desk inside the foyer. She knocked and waved till she attracted his attention, inspecting her appearance in the glass during the time it took for the man to stride over.

The wrap-around silk dress suited her both in colour and style, but she was dismayed at the obvious dark shadows under her eyes. With her recent weight loss she looked all eyes and cheekbones, particularly with her hair scraped back into a tight roll. But it was the image she wanted, that of a mature, confident woman, not some silly young sex-starved widow.

'Yes?' the guard asked abruptly, once he had unlocked and swung open one of the glass doors.

Rhea swallowed. 'My name is Mrs Petrovic, Rhea

Petrovic. I'd like to see Mr Chase—I believe he's working here today.'

'Is he expecting you, Mrs Petrovic?'

'No, but I'm sure he'll see me. If you just tell me which floor he's——'

'I'll have to check,' he interrupted firmly.

'Oh . . . Yes . . . Yes, of course.'

The guard ushered her inside before leaving her to glance agitatedly around the spacious foyer while he marched over to the reception desk. Nerves crowded into Rhea's stomach as he made a brief telephone call.

'It's OK, Mrs Petrovic,' the man called over. 'Mr Chase's secretary said you could go right up. Seventeenth floor. His office is directly opposite the elevator doors.'

Rhea's heart sank. His secretary . . . She hadn't anticipated he would be working with someone. She had wanted to see him alone.

The best laid plans of mice and men, she muttered to herself as she walked over to the one lift that showed a red light above. She punched the seventeen, noting that it was the the highest floor—other than the penthouse. The doors shot back straight away. She sighed. Not even a minute's respite in which to gather her composure.

The ride up was as smooth as the building, and the man who owned it, with Rhea fortifying herself with clichés all the way. Nothing ventured, nothing gained . . . Every cloud has a silver lining . . . Anything worth having is worth fighting for . . .

When the doors slid back at the seventeenth floor she was far from confident. But she tried not to look it, walking purposefully across the bouncy green carpet and pushing through another set of swinging glass doors with 'Chase Investments' gilded on them. The luxurious reception area was empty, bringing a further rush of uncertainty.

Suddenly the heavy wooden door directly in front of her opened, and Rhea's heart turned over in her chest as a beautiful young woman walked through. Stephen's secretary. she concluded. But also the same beautiful young woman Rhea had seen him with in the coffee lounge.

Immediately, dark thoughts swamped her mind. Dark, jealous thoughts. So! He was working night and day, was he? How convenient, when his bedroom was one floor up from his office and his secretary was doing a lot more than type his letters!

Just as swiftly Rhea pulled herself up short. No! She was not going to do this any more, jump to conclusions about Stephen without proof. OK, so he might have slept with his secretary at one time. Why not? He was single, and she was . . . *married*!

Rhea gaped at the engagement and wedding rings on the girl's left hand as she reached up to push a blonde curl back from her forehead.

'Mrs Petrovic?' the secretary was saying with a warm smile. 'I'm Melanie Roberts, Stephen's secretary. Do come inside . . . Stephen wasn't here when your message came through. He'd just gone upstairs to have a shower and a shave, but he won't be long. Poor man, he was working most of last night on a presentation he's making tomorrow in Brisbane.'

She gave Rhea a surveying look as she showed her into an expansive office, but there was not a hint of the competitive bitchiness in her manner that Rhea might have expected.

'Please . . .' Melanie pulled out a comfortable chair for Rhea to sit in, then settled herself in the smaller of the two swivel-chairs behind the huge and very cluttered desk that dominated the room.

'It's a mess, isn't it?' the secretary smiled as she saw Rhea's glance. 'But Stephen knows where everything is. If I tidy it up too much, I'm in real trouble!'

Rhea nodded and swallowed. The girl was very natural. And very beautiful.

She gradually became aware that she was being stared at also. She blinked her surprise.

'Mrs Petrovic . . .' Melanie began.

'Yes?'

The secretary glanced a little nervously at the open door. 'I hope you won't take offence, but I must speak out now that I have the chance.'

'About . . . about what?'

'About you . . . and Stephen.'

Rhea stiffened. How on earth would this girl know anything about her and Stephen, unless he had confided their brief affair?

'Oh, please, don't go thinking Stephen has been talking about any personal relationship you and he might have, because he hasn't. He keeps his private life private. I'm putting two and two together here, merely because I know him so well . . .'

Rhea tried not to let her feelings show on her face.

'I've worked for Stephen for five years,' Melanie went on. 'He's like a big brother to me. He gave me away at my wedding last year because my father died some years back. See this beautiful watch? He gave that to me after I came back from my honeymoon because he missed me so much . . .'

She paused, letting her words sink in.

'I care about my boss, Mrs Petrovic,' she added sincerely. 'And I know his moods very well. I know when he's happy, or sad. I certainly know when he's deeply disturbed. You see, when he's troubled in any way, he works. Not that he doesn't work long hours normally, but when he's really upset he's like a demon. In the past, the reason for his workaholic bursts has always been some bad business deal. Believe me when I tell you this is the first time a woman has been the cause . . .'

Rhea held her breath.

'. . . and I think that woman is you, Mrs Petrovic.'

'But . . . how can you . . .?'

'Stephen has naturally talked to me about his problems with Laura, and how things have changed for the better since he followed your advice about the local school. So in that context he has spoken of you quite often, and I couldn't help but notice the way he looked every time your name was mentioned. You should have seen his face when he told me about the way you set him straight the day Laura ran away!'

Rhea groaned as she remembered.

'Please don't be embarrassed,' the girl insisted. 'He admired you for it! There haven't been many women, believe me, who've told him what to do and where to go. They're usually only too willing to fall at his feet! Then one day last month I flew with him to Brisbane on business and he had the biggest grin on his face. I asked him what coup he'd managed, but he shook his head, then burst out with, "She's a widow, Melanie! A widow!" as if all his birthdays had come at once. I knew then, Mrs Petrovic, that Stephen had finally fallen in love.' She slanted Rhea a hopeful look. 'I only hope that your coming here today means you love him just as much.'

Rhea wasn't sure what to say, her heart leaping with joy and relief. Till another, more cynical train of thought took over. Did this girl know her boss that well? Did anyone know *anyone* that well? Couldn't Stephen's pleasure have been an egotistical burst of triumph at finding out a chink in the armour of the one woman who had dared to spurn him? She would have been a challenge for him, just like a difficult business deal. And now he was in a black mood because things had not worked out his way.

The distinctive sound of lift doors swishing open punctuated the quiet air of the deserted building.

'There's Stephen now,' Melanie said as she stood up. 'Please don't mention that I said anything, Mrs Petrovic,' she whispered urgently. 'He'd be furious with me!'

The secretary fell silent as her boss breezed into his office. 'That feels better. One more hour should see us——' Stephen broke off, staring with his mouth open at Rhea.

She got slowly to her feet, unable to stop staring back at him. Somehow during their two weeks' separation she had been so engaged in realising how deeply she loved him that she had almost forgotten the intensity of the attraction between them.

Immediately, it had a tendency to blot out everything else for her. Her eyes drank him in hungrily, from the still damp black waves curving around his finely shaped head down to his impressively proportioned body, clad all too revealingly in a chest-hugging black sports shirt and white canvas shorts. He didn't even have anything on his feet.

If only his secretary was right, Rhea thought breathlessly. If only he did love her! She swayed on her feet, clutching at the arm of the chair to steady herself.

Stephen was the first to pull himself together. 'Rhea? What are you doing here?' he said sharply. 'Is there something wrong at home? Emily? The dogs?'

Rhea's heart sank. How telling that he would assume her only reason for visiting him would be some outside problem!

Tears flooded her eyes, making her look down in a fluster of embarrassment. She hadn't realised how strung up she was, how she had been holding herself together with the mad hope that he would be overjoyed to see her. Yet here he was, coldly asking her if some crisis had forced her to ask him for help once more.

The depressing realisation of dreams shattering sent the tears spilling over her eyes and down her cheeks in an unchecked flood. 'Oh, God!' she sobbed, her trembling hands moving up to hide her face.

Then somehow she *was* in his arms, though perhaps not quite as she had dreamt. He was holding her with obvious reluctance, an angry tension in the hands that were patting her head and back.

'There, there,' he muttered. 'Don't cry . . . For pity's sake, don't cry!'

'I'm sorry,' she choked, not even knowing what she was saying sorry for. 'Sorry . . .'

Stephen sighed, then gathered her more gently to him, holding her wet face against his chest. 'Hush! Don't try to talk,' he soothed. 'Be still . . . Hush!'

He must have mouthed something to his secretary, or made signals, for when at last Rhea calmed, the sobs dying away, she pulled back and glanced around to see the office was empty.

'I sent Melanie home,' he remarked quietly, leaning over to pull a handful of tissues from a box on his desk. 'Here . . .'

Rhea wiped up the tears, noting ruefully that when she did so quite a bit of mascara came too. 'I must look a mess,' she muttered, her eyes still downcast. Stephen's reluctance to hold her had not escaped her notice. He had merely been doing the gentlemanly thing in comforting her, the only thing he could do when a woman burst into tears in front of him.

Her heart was shrivelling up further by the minute. 'I'm sorry,' she repeated dully.

'For what, Rhea? came his weary words.

When she finally lifted her chin to look at him he had moved away from her to stand behind his desk, eyeing her with a grim wariness. It struck her quite forcibly that he looked like a man who was hurting as much as she was. Her stomach twisted with a last stab of desperate hope and she sought frantically for the right words.

'For . . . for a lot of things,' she said haltingly.

'Oh?' He adopted a closed expression and moved to sit down in the large black leather chair. He indicated the chair she had used earlier. 'Then perhaps you should sit down, Rhea, and explain them to me.'

Rhea swallowed and did so, lifting eyes that belied the battery of butterflies in her stomach. She hated seeing the raw pain in his face, yet clutched comfort from it. Pain usually meant that at some time there had been deep emotion involved, maybe the love her mother and his secretary had suggested. If so, Rhea hoped she wasn't too late to salvage some of it.

'I'm sorry,' she began, 'for the way I've treated you. I . . . I know I've behaved very badly. I shouldn't have lied to you about being married, and I know it looks as if I was only using you for sex. But you have to understand, Stephen, I'm not very experienced where men are concerned. A man like you . . . You frightened me, Stephen. Just look at you! Look at this place . . . You're rich and successful. You could have any woman you wanted . . .'

She sighed, not sure she was saying the right things, his increasingly strained face not giving her any indication that she was getting through to him. 'I . . . I couldn't imagine you'd really want me, certainly not for anything else except sex. I . . . I know I misjudged you . . . But it isn't true that I don't like or respect you, Stephen. I do. More than that. I . . . I . . .' She lifted a trembling hand to her temple, trying to still the throbbing in her head, feeling she was putting everything very badly.

She clung on to her mother's words—'What have you got to lose?'—and looked the darkly frowning man opposite her straight in the eye. 'I love you, Stephen. Terribly.'

He froze, then snapped forward in the chair, closing

his eyes briefly before opening them to reveal an unutterable weariness. He shook his head. 'I don't think so, Rhea.'

For a second, Rhea could not believe what she had heard. 'But . . . but I do!' she protested.

'No.' He set anguished eyes upon her. 'You're confusing sex with love. It's easily done—I did it myself once. But it doesn't last. It isn't real.'

'No, Stephen, you're wrong. Wrong!' She was on her feet and her hands gripped the side of his desk. 'I admit I thought it was just a physical attraction too—at first. My response to you really shocked me.'

He looked confused. '*Shocked* you?'

'Yes, shocked me.'

'That seems a trifle melodramatic, Rhea,' he said with undisguised scepticism.

'Oh, God . . . can't you see? Haven't you realised? Not only are you the first lover I've ever taken, Stephen, but you're the first man I've ever even wanted. You're the first man who's ever given me . . . satisfaction.'

Now he was on his feet, looking at her across the desk with total exasperation. 'For God's sake, Rhea, do you expect me to believe that? You were married for five years! You must have enjoyed sleeping with your husband at least once!'

'No, Stephen, *never*! I loved my husband, but not as a woman should love a man. He was more of a father figure to me. Sex was something I did for him, not for myself. That was why after his death I never sought involvement with a man. I couldn't stand the thought of having to . . . to . . .'

She threw him a beseeching look. 'Don't you

understand what I'm saying? When I met you and wanted you so much, I *was* shocked. I didn't make any connection between these alien, unexpected desires and love, because I'd never felt that type of love before. Love for me had always been something quiet, steady . . . safe. Not instant and wild and uncontrollable! When you burst into my life I seemed in danger of losing the peaceful secure life that I'd battled long and hard for. I fought my feelings like crazy, lying to you, lying to myself. I . . . I know I've made a mess of things, Stephen, but I do love you. So much that the thought of life without you is unbearable.'

All the time she had been speaking he had stared at her, his face a mixture of wonder and wariness. For what seemed an interminable span of time, a breathless silence hung in the air, till at last Stephen expelled a ragged sigh. 'You do realise, Rhea, that what you've just said has a flaw in logic. You say you love me. But given your history, it's equally possible that now you've discovered the pleasure, the joy of sex, it's *that* that you've been missing. Not me.'

'How can you say that?' Rhea cried. 'I could go to bed with any number of men. I wouldn't need to come here today with my heart on my sleeve, my pride in shreds. Oh, Stephen, why don't you just say you don't love me? That's the bottom line, isn't it?'

She turned away, her despair reaching such mammoth proportions that as she took a step the room swirled before her blurring eyes. She made a grab for the chair, sending it toppling over, a whimpering cry rushing from her lungs as the floor started rising towards her.

Stephen caught her just before she hit the carpet, sinking to the floor with her and cradling her in his arms. 'Not love you?' he rasped as she struggled back from the threatening blackness to blink dazedly up into his torn face. 'Not love you?' he repeated, stretching out with his back against the desk, curling her body up in his lap and arms. 'Oh, my darling Rhea, my sweet darling Rhea . . . You're the only woman I've ever loved. Don't you know that?'

She could only stare up at him, hardly daring to believe those longed-for words.

'I was madly attracted to you right from that first day in the church,' he sighed. 'There you were, a vision of loveliness sitting at that organ, your face a perfect oval of innocence, this virginal quality seemingly at odds with the sensual abandonment of your beautiful hair. I wanted to touch it, and you, very badly . . .'

He reached around the back of her head, pulling the pins from her hair, letting the waves cascade over his arm. Her breath caught in her throat as he began spreading her hair out, his fingers running through it with an unconscious eroticism.

'It gave me an awful jolt,' he was saying, 'when I realised you were a married woman with a child. It shattered all my plans. In my mind I already had you in my bed, determined to taste all the promise your glances bespoke. My God, Rhea, do you realise how you looked at me that day? It was like nothing I've ever experienced before. One moment your eyes were filled with a yearning, a passion that was totally compelling. And then . . . such alarm, such fear. In a way, it was almost a relief to find out you were spoken for. I told myself later I'd imagined your desire, that you'd been amazed perhaps that I tried to pick you up, disgusted even. That was certainly verified later when I came to get Laura . . . You have to admit I did disgust you over Laura.'

'I was wrong,' Rhea whispered, unable to say more. She wished he would stop playing with her hair, stop letting his fingertips brush against her neck. She felt as if her skin were burning up. Her clothes were sticking to her.

'Not totally wrong,' Stephen surprised her by saying. 'I have been a selfish man, pleasing no other person in my life but myself. I wanted money, success, power. And relationships without strings, without commitment. I only ever took out independent career women, women whom I would never be tempted to fall in love with . . .'

He began untying the belt that secured her wrap-around dress, making her throat dry up completely. Her heart began to thud against the walls of her chest, making her breasts rise and fall with telling speed.

'I suppose, after Laura's mother, I had a somewhat cynical attitude towards love. I was deeply hurt by the way she treated me, convincing me she loved me and then dumping me cold. I was only twenty-one at the time. Our dear Naomi was a very experienced thirty-seven.'

'Thirty-*seven*?' Rhea sat up straight, her astonishment having the effect of halting Stephen's fingers on her belt, which was not her intention.

'She looked a well-preserved twenty-eight when I

met her,' he explained. 'It was during the last year of my economics-law degree. I had a part-time job in a stockbrokers' firm. Naomi was one of their hot-shot investment advisers. Being young and naïve—and presumably virile—I was the perfect candidate as the father of her planned child. Shortly after our brief affair she just disappeared, resigned from the company and left, leaving no forwarding address. No farewell tears, no goodbye, no telling stupid old Stevie boy he was about to become a daddy. Naomi wasn't large on sharing, it seemed.'

Rhea heard the bitterness in his voice and realised that Naomi Hatfield's desertion had affected him very deeply. No wonder he was so hurt by that night at the penthouse! It would have looked as if the two women in his life he had really cared about were only interested in his body.

'Not like *you*,' he rasped, tipping her back into the crook of his arm. 'You're all woman, Rhea—giving, loving, warm. But still sexy . . . very sexy . . .' He bent to kiss her, their tongues meeting in an explosion of longing. 'I knew I was in love with you,' he murmured into her trembling mouth, 'when I kept getting so angry with you. I wanted you to love me back, but I was so sure you despised me.'

He lifted his mouth away to look down at her, frustration in his eyes. 'Remember when you were at my place and I received a phone call? It was from a woman named Madeline, an actress I'd been seeing last year.'

'Yes,' Rhea nodded, 'I know about Madeline.'

'You do?'

Rhea had realised earlier on, when Stephen had accused her of confusing sex with love, that she could never tell him about the two times she had seen him before they officially met. He might not understand the subtleties behind her instant attraction. He would only see lust. So she smiled softly and said, 'Laura told Emily, who told me.'

'Women!' groaned Stephen.

'You don't seem to be able to do without them,' she said teasingly, but the comment made him frown.

'You don't still think me some kind of Casanova, Rhea, do you?'

'I don't care what you've been, Stephen,' she murmured understandingly. 'It's what you're going to be I'm interested in.'

She could see, though, that her answer irritated him. 'But I never was that type of man. Yes, there were women — I admit that. I'm a normal male. But not all that many women, and only one at a time. As I told you once before, I'm a busy man. Madeline was the only female in my life before you came into it, and we had already ended our relationship, though I see now that Madeline found this hard to accept. However, when I found out about Laura, Madeline had told me she had little patience with children.'

He sighed. 'Perhaps I should have broken off all contact with her straight away, but I needed some sort of support. Finding out about Naomi and Laura had been a shock. My life seemed one mad rush to fit everything in, and to be truthful I was depressed over Laura's attitude. I thought she hated me and would be happier away from me. Madeline sounded as if she really cared when she suggested boarding school. But when I met you and saw what a truly caring woman thought about the situation I realised she'd just been manipulating things for her own advantage, that she hadn't come to terms with our new friendship, and I sent her packing.'

'Yet you went out with her again,' Rhea inserted quietly.

'Strictly a platonic date, I assure you. I wouldn't even have agreed to that if a certain lady hadn't just rejected me rather brutally.'

A guilty blush flamed into her face.

'A lady I loved quite desperately.' He stroked her cheek and kissed her again before letting his hand drift down to her waist.

Rhea suppressed a groan. Dared she take his hand in hers and move it to her aching breast? No, no, she couldn't. He would think she only wanted sex from him.

But there was no need for her to do anything, for he was in tune with her desires, his fingers moving to her belt to complete what he had begun an eternity ago.

'You will marry me, won't you?' he whispered as he flicked the silk ties to either side of her body.

Rhea could only blink in amazement at his words. That he loved her had completed most of her dream. To have him ask her to marry him was almost too much.

A quivering sigh fluttered from her lips as she pressed her eyes shut. When she opened them to look at Stephen he was busily concentrating on peeling back her dress.

Rhea had chosen her underwear that day without daring to investigate why, the matching set having been part of her trousseau. But she had never worn them.

They had lain in a drawer, waiting, so it seemed now, for the moment when she would wear them for the man she loved. And they were indeed sexy garments, the ivory silk petticoat lending a warm glow to her softly tanned skin, the inserts of lace giving tempting glimpses of the womanly lushness of her body. Stephen's gaze ran hungrily over her body, bringing an even warmer glow.

'You haven't given me an answer,' he said thickly.

'Yes,' she whispered when one of his hands began tracing the swollen curves of her breasts, her back arching to press them more firmly into his palm. He groaned and moved his hand in erotic circles, rubbing her nipples into agonisingly hard peaks. 'Yes,' she repeated on a sob of pleasure.

As always Stephen took his time, sliding the straps from her shoulders with almost annoying slowness, his fingers brushing her bare skin as they attended to the front clasp on her bra. This he discarded, but he left the petticoat to fall around her hips, making no attempt to strip her further. Rhea noted with amazement that she even still had her shoes on.

She kicked them off, then twisted in his lap till she faced him, sliding her bare arms up around his neck. 'Love me, Stephen,' she whispered shakily, hoping he wouldn't misunderstand. But she wanted him, *needed* him at that moment, more than she had ever done.

He dragged in a shuddering breath, then suddenly yanked her hard against him, kissing her long and deep till they were both breathless. Rhea was momentarily worried when he set her aside, but when he began stripping with almost indecent haste she threw any remaining qualms and inhibitions out of the window and wriggled out of the rest of her clothes.

His naked form was beside hers on the floor within seconds, drawing her back on to his lap, fitting his throbbing hardness into her body with a forceful and almost shocking speed. Rough hands wrapped her legs around his hips, then he was rocking her back and forth in a passionate, primitive mating that was unlike any Rhea had ever conceived of. It was so much more overwhelming because she knew Stephen was normally a lover of the subtle, the slow, a true savourer of sensual pleasure.

But this was not like that. This was a demonstration of a raw, naked emotion that was beyond any elongated, erotic exploration. This was a physical union at its most basic, a man taking a woman with no thought of expertise, no idea of delaying satisfaction till every vestige of delight had been teased from it. This was a compelling, instinctive response to a deep and true love, a love that demanded not so much a making love, but a making one.

It underlined to Rhea the intense nature of Stephen's feelings. With her at this moment he could not be the man he usually was; he could not control, or direct, or wait . . .

The realisation of such a compulsive need exploded through her like the ultimate intoxication, increasing her own already inflamed desire. Her mouth sought his with a fierce response, her nails digging into his back as she moved with him, wildly, savagely, quickly bringing about a shuddering mutual release of soul-shattering intensity. They sagged into each other, the melding of

their flesh completed, only their minds left to wonder
dazedly as they drew back to gaze at each other in an
awestruck silence, their chests still heaving with the
effort of their spent passion.

At last Stephen's hand reached out to push some
madly tangled locks of hair from her face. 'If it's always
going to be like this,' he choked out, 'then I'll be dead
within a week!'

With a shuddering sigh they both sank to the floor,
holding and stroking each other into a calmer state in an
almost shocked silence.

'Stephen,' Rhea whispered at last.

'Hmm?'

'I . . . I hate to bring this up, at such a time . . . but I
think I should mention it . . .'

'What?'

'The first time we made love, it was almost
perfectly safe. And this time too . . . But if we don't
take precautions soon . . .'

She lifted her head from his chest to see the smile
form on his face. 'You don't mind if I get pregnant?'

'What do you think, Mrs Chase?' he murmured,
drawing her back down to him. 'Where's Emily?' he
asked, distracting her with the change of subject.

'Staying with her grandmother for a couple of days.'

'Then you can stay with me tonight? All night?'

Rhea should have got over blushing by now, but it
seemed she hadn't. 'Yes,' she whispered, hiding her face
at the base of his neck.

Stephen scrambled to his feet, lifting her naked body
into his arms and carrying her from the office.

'Where are we going?' she gasped.

'Upstairs to bed,' he told her as he pushed through the glass doors with his elbow. 'I'm too old for this floor nonsense.'

'But . . . but what about your work? Melanie said you were going to Brisbane tomorrow.'

'Postponed as of now!'

She giggled as he directed her big toe to press the button for the penthouse lift, linking her arms tightly around his neck while he angled her body into the small enclosed space. Rhea was enjoying the sensation of being held naked against his equally naked body. It made her feel tiny and vulnerable and female, his strong arms carrying her as though she were a feather.

But along with these new feelings of submissive pleasure was a sense of feminine power. Stephen loved her, loved her and wanted her with a passion he could scarcely control. Her new womanly instincts told her that she only had to slide her skin suggestively against his, give him a certain look and he would be set upon a path from which there was no drawing back.

As the doors slid shut to enclose them in a temporary cocoon, Rhea glanced up at Stephen through smoky, half-closed eyes. She twisted slightly in his arms so that her still hard nipple grazed his. 'You know, Stephen,' she whispered huskily, 'I've never made love in an elevator . . .'

CHAPTER FIFTEEN

RHEA was running late. Which was forgivable, since she was the bride. But Emily and Laura were getting agitated at her constant checking that everything was perfect with her appearance.

'Come on, Mum,' Emily urged. 'Dad will be having a pink fit if we're not at the church soon!'

Rhea warmed to the way her daughter had already accepted Stephen as her stepfather, despite only one month having gone by since they had announced their engagement.

'Yes, Rhea,' Bill chimed in, 'it's time we left, but may I say before we do how radiant you look?'

Rhea's mirror agreed. There was a bloom in her cheeks that made her look like the traditional blushing bride, though the image was certainly helped by the dress she had made. It was an elaborate gown in dazzling white satin, with a fitted, off-the-shoulder bodice, a nipped-in waist and a wide flouncing skirt. The veil was long at the back with a delicate orange-blossom head-piece and a shorter veil covering her face.

Rhea had rejected any idea of dressing down for her second wedding. It was Stephen's first, and the girls had been keen to be proper bridesmaids.

'I think she's the most beautiful bride in the whole world,' breathed Laura, gazing up at her soon-to-be mother in loving awe.

Emotion curled around Rhea's heart, bringing a lump to her throat. 'Not as beautiful as my two bridesmaids,' she complimented. Emily looked startlingly grown-up in floor-length lilac chiffon; Laura, like a Dresden doll in the same style in sweetest pink. Both had matching picture hats and flowers.

'If we don't leave now, Rhea,' Bill warned, 'I'll have to answer to your mother!'

She smiled at her stepfather, linking her arm through his and letting him lead her outside, the girls rushing forward to carry the train of her veil. 'Have I ever told you I love you?' she whispered to him as he helped her into the bridal car.

His glance carried shock, then a wealth of emotion. He made no reply, just took and patted her hand, clearly unable to speak.

The church looked marvellous, spruced up by a coat of white paint paid for by Stephen. The grounds had benefited too, having been mown and tidied by his gardener the day before.

Rhea was not surprised to see several reporters waiting for her in the churchyard, resigning herself to the fact she was marrying a man of considerable standing. Though, from what she had seen of Stephen, he was not a flaunter of his fame and fortune, keeping a low-key profile as much as possible. A lover of publicity would certainly not have chosen to be married in Bangaloo Creek Church.

But as the reporters crowded forward, snapping photographs and jotting down notes, Rhea realised that being Mrs Stephen Chase would take some getting used to. Yet she was not in any way nervous about this marriage, a fact that would have surprised the Rhea of a few months ago. She had changed in so many ways since meeting and loving Stephen, feeling much more confident in herself as a person and a woman.

The bridal chorus started up as soon as she appeared in the doorway, a young man playing the organ. Stephen had hired him with the same efficiency he had done everything in the meagre four weeks they had had to make all the arrangements. His capacity for hard work and getting things done was a bit overwhelming, not to mention the miles he covered most weeks. He was always going here, flying there on some business deal or other. But at least it was mostly in Australia, rarely overseas. And, to be honest, Rhea had no wish to change him. She loved Stephen as he was, human dynamo and all. And Emily adored him, never more so than on the day after their engagement when he had shown up with the most beautiful chestnut pony Rhea had ever seen.

The pony hadn't been his only purchase that day either. Her old van was mysteriously whisked away, with a brand new white sedan taking its place. Stephen had brushed aside any objection with a firm look, then a seductive kiss. 'Can't have my fiancée breaking down on one of these lonely roads, can I?' he said reasonably.

Rhea sighed contentedly with her memories, then looked down the aisle, catching her breath as Stephen turned to gaze back down at her. How handsome he looked! How wonderful! How . . . *nervous*?

The thought made her smile. Her Stephen—nervous? The same Stephen who had already put her farm up for auction, moved her goats to his place, had proper kennels built for the dogs and brought his parents down to mind the children while they went on the honeymoon he had booked in Tahiti?

But nervous he most certainly looked.

She started the slow walk down the aisle, throwing smiles at all the people who had come to wish her well. She saved a special beam for Stephen's parents, who were a delightful old couple, and seemed to genuinely like her.

'What rubbish!' Stephen had snapped when she had dared voice her worry that they might think her not good enough for him. 'I'm a simple farm boy myself. No airs and graces about my family!'

And there weren't, Rhea agreed as she cast a warm eye over his three brothers and two sisters, who had come to the wedding, with spouses and countless children in tow. If Stephen was as potent as his siblings Rhea was going to be kept busy!

Which thought had her gently touch her stomach behind her bouquet of flowers. She was only a couple of days late, but there was no doubt in her mind that she had already conceived Stephen's child. Despite his busy schedule his passion for her had not waned. It took her breath away to think of the many times they had made love already, not to mention the mad places!

As she approached the altar she caught a glimpse of her mother out of the corner of her eye, looking burstingly happy. Rhea grinned at her before bringing her attention back to Stephen.

For a second, he seemed taken aback by her unabashed happiness, but then the sight of his bride, smiling widely up at him, broke his strain, and he grinned back at her.

He took her arm quite eagerly and they turned together to face the priest.

'We are gathered together here . . .'

Rhea darted a glance up at Stephen as the words rolled over them, drawing his gaze. They looked into each other's eyes, the mutual emotion in their depths echoing the words of the ceremony.

'Stephen Richard, wilt thou have this woman to thy wedded wife . . .? Wilt thou love her, comfort her, honour, and keep her in sickness and in health; and, foresaking all other, keep thee only unto her, so long as ye both shall live?'

His eyes caressed her as he said, 'I will.'

'Rhea Catherine, wilt thou have this man to thy wedded husband . . .'

It was a beautiful simple ceremony ending with the traditional, 'I pronounce that they be man and wife together.'

Then the priest cleared his throat. 'Er . . . You may kiss the bride.'

Stephen turned and slowly lifted her veil, his face having taken on a more serious expression. 'I love you, Rhea,' he murmured.

His mouth met hers, sweetly, reverentially, yet smouldering with an impatient, barely contained passion. Rhea melted against him, knowing that what they had together was something so special that not even death would bring a halt to it. As long as their children and their children's children lived, they would be a testimony to a love that was as rare as the most priceless jewel, a love that encompassed all that a man and woman could ever possibly hope for.

It was certainly all that Rhea had hoped for, she thought blissfully as her lips parted and she began to kiss him back.

HISTORICAL

CHRISTMAS

STORIES · 1991

Bring back heartwarming memories of Christmas past,
with Historical Christmas Stories 1991, a collection of
romantic stories by three popular authors:

Christmas Yet To Come
by Lynda Trent

A Season of Joy
by Caryn Cameron

Fortune's Gift
by DeLoras Scott

A perfect Christmas gift!

HARLEQUIN
Romance

A Christmas tradition . . .

Imagine spending Christmas in New
Orleans with a blind stranger and his aged
guide dog—when you're supposed to be
there on your honeymoon!
#3163 Every Kind of Heaven
by Bethany Campbell

Imagine spending Christmas with a man
you once "married"—in a mock ceremony
at the age of eight!
#3166 The Forgetful Bride
by Debbie Macomber

*Available in December 1991, wherever
Harlequin books are sold.*

RXM

Take 4 bestselling love stories FREE

Plus get a FREE surprise gift!

Special Limited-time Offer

Mail to Harlequin Reader Service®

In the U.S.	In Canada
3010 Walden Avenue	P.O. Box 609
P.O. Box 1867	Fort Erie, Ontario
Buffalo, N.Y. 14269-1867	L2A 5X3

YES! Please send me 4 free Harlequin Presents® novels and my free surprise gift. Then send me 6 brand-new novels every month, which I will receive months before they appear in bookstores. Bill me at the low price of $2.49* each—a savings of 30¢ apiece off cover prices. There are no shipping, handling or other hidden costs. I understand that accepting the books and gift places me under no obligation ever to buy any books. I can always return a shipment and cancel at any time. Even if I never buy another book from Harlequin, the 4 free books and the surprise gift are mine to keep forever.

*Offer slightly different in Canada—$2.49 per book plus 69¢ per shipment for delivery. Canadian residents add applicable federal and provincial sales tax. Sales tax applicable in N.Y.

106 BPA ADLZ   306 BPA ADMF

Name	(PLEASE PRINT)	
Address		Apt. No.
City	State/Prov.	Zip/Postal Code

This offer is limited to one order per household and not valid to present Harlequin Presents® subscribers. Terms and prices are subject to change.

PRES-91   © 1990 Harlequin Enterprises Limited